THE BOOK OF COLORS

THE

BOOK OF COLORS

Raymond Barfield

UNBRIDLED BOOKS

This is a work of fiction. The names, characters, places and incidents are either the product of the author's imagination or are used fictitiously, and any resemblance to actual persons living or dead, business establishments, events, or locales is entirely coincidental.

UNBRIDLED BOOKS

Library of Congress Cataloging-in-Publication Data
Barfield, Raymond, 1964-
The book of colors / by Raymond Barfield. -- First edition.
pages ; cm
ISBN 978-1-60953-115-7 (softcover)
1. Pregnant women--Tennessee--Memphis--Fiction. 2. Self-actualization (Psychology) in women--Fiction. 3. Self-realization in women--Fiction. I. Title.
PS3602.A77536B66 2015
813'.6--dc23
2014047940

1 3 5 7 9 10 8 6 4 2

Book Design by SH • CV

First Printing

For Alexandra

THE
BOOK OF COLORS

Black Rose on a White Deathbed

Rose called out to me.

"Yslea. Yslea, are you there?"

"I'm here."

"I can't feel my feet again."

"You been dreaming?"

"No. I been thinking."

"What about?"

"Big things. Nothing to worry your mind about."

"What big things?"

"Don't mind me."

"You want me to rub your feet?"

"Maybe in a while."

I sat down by Rose's bed, hoping dinner cooked before the stove stopped working, and I rubbed my belly, round under the flowers of my dress. My belly button had smoothed out in the past few weeks.

I think about big things as much as anyone, maybe more, even though I almost never talk to anyone about them. I go to bed thinking about them. Wake up thinking about them. My baby for example. While it was growing it was so calm it scared me sometimes. I used to know girls who'd wake up in the middle of the night with a foot stuck in their ribs and they'd laugh telling about it. I wanted my baby to do that, just to say hello.

Rose looked up from her bed and sniffed around a little bit. "What you cooking tonight, Yslea?"

It was a wonder she could still smell with all the bug spray in her room. She had me spray it at least twice a day. "Jimmy brought pork chops from work."

"Those gray ones?"

"They taste the same once they're cooked. He gets them half price."

"I'm not complaining. I'm not hungry anyway." Rose relaxed into her pillow. That was about the only thing to tell you she was tense—watching her relax. She couldn't move much on her own. Not that she was so big anymore. She was before, but she stopped eating enough to stay big. Somehow she still seemed big when you thought about her, though.

My own bigness was new. That was the difference. If you looked at me you'd think I was small, even though my belly had started filling up my lap. I never used to think much about having a body until this other body started growing inside mine. I just wished it'd move more. I wondered what it was gonna do when it got into the world and just lay there. That's not how the world works.

When Rose started snoring I watched her sleeping like I sometimes did to get used to how she'd look when she's dead. I hadn't seen many dead people. I needed to not be scared, and Jimmy wasn't much good except for meat from the butcher shop. And if I ever got thin again, for love. But I wasn't sure what I wanted anymore.

I hadn't been with Rose long. A few months. To start with, Rose didn't know a thing about me but she brought me in as a favor to Jimmy, even though she didn't think much of Jimmy. Most likely at first she was more interested in the little thing growing in me than in me or Jimmy. That's okay. Once I moved in we got on so well she asked me to be the one to dress her when she died.

I'd only been living with Jimmy next door for a couple of months when I figured out I was pregnant, but I'd known him for a while before I moved in and I'd see Rose on her porch. I agreed to dress her when she died because I figure that if a baby can grow from nothing in that time so can that kind of relation between me and Rose.

They say you shouldn't eat fried foods when you're pregnant, but that's the only way to get the pork chops cooked since the oven in the house didn't work so well, probably because Rose always used it too much in the winter to heat the house.

The other thing I worried about was Rose's bug spray. They say you shouldn't be around bug spray if you're pregnant. For someone who kept saying God is in control of the world Rose sure was scared of bugs. I asked her about it and she said she once woke up with a roach attached to her ear. I didn't know roaches did that, although I did hear once of a baby dying when a roach crawled into its windpipe. That might do it. Maybe it's better to be around bug spray than to have a roach crawl into your child's mouth. At least that's what I told myself.

Dinnertime is one of the times the train comes by. It's loud enough to stir up a valley of dry bones, but Rose always slept right through it. I've always wondered at what people can get used to. A person growing inside you. Or the idea that you might just up and die.

Even though I'm not a Catholic I started going to the Catholic church down the street. All sorts of people come. It's the strangest time of my week when people who I might not even be able to get into their offices kneel down beside me and we eat the flesh and drink the blood of God and I always leave feeling clean and happy. The only other time I feel that way is when I'm reading Robinson Crusoe, which is the book I own.

The Sofa People

The first time I saw Rose was the first time I saw Jimmy. They were sitting on their porches, Rose on hers, Jimmy on his. Their neighbor Layla was there too sitting on her porch as far away from Jimmy and Rose as she could sit with her girl Ambrosia cross-legged rocking like she always does, slowly turning the pages of her little cardboard book of colors like she always does.

The way their three little row houses sort of leaned in toward each other and the way the paint peeled and some of the windows were covered with cardboard, the row might as easily have been empty. But those folk not talking, just feeling what little breeze there was, each one of them with a ragged sofa on their porch—it was better than trudging along the train track ready to die of thirst and seeing nothing but more track.

"Can you spare a glass of water?" I asked and I had my hands on the post and I see now that I tried to look good for the man Jimmy, innocent for the old woman Rose, and interested only in water for the young woman Layla until I had things figured out. Not that I thought of it that way at the time, but my brain sort of chatters to me all the time if I'm not paying attention to something like reading my book or cutting an onion, which is fine if I'm just remembering things but it gets in the way sometimes if I'm trying to listen to a sermon or a radio show because it's always like two people are talking at the same time.

Rose wiped her face but Jimmy answered first with his thumb pointing toward the back screen door. "Glass's inside."

If I only had a second to describe the world or tell a story I'd say that's how it came about that somebody started growing inside me. But things seemed leisurely in those days since I had almost nothing else to do.

So I went on inside. I thought he'd said "glasses" but he said "glass's" and I could only find one glass and it was dirty so if he didn't have that man's look about him I'd have drunk straight from the faucet.

The water was tepid. I should have let it run longer and bubble up from the cooler parts below Memphis but I was thirsty. I looked around. Was I glad that I didn't see any signs of a woman? It didn't really occur to me that way at the time, but maybe. That's what I mean about the chatter.

The sofas outside were the colors of a squash (Rose's), a green bean (Jimmy's), and a fresh-dug yam (Layla's). They were tilted but stable like everything else in my life at the time.

Jimmy's house was a bone of a house lodged between two houses that were bones of houses. I thought as I left that first day and almost stepped into the mess of a dead raccoon sprawled on the railroad track that their houses were like three broken ribs stuck off to the side of the railroad spine.

So I got my water and took a couple of eyefuls of Jimmy's spare little shack, all dull gray, covered in faded old sheets to keep the stuffing of various things in, and out of the drab background the chemical-blue eye of a computer screen with its soft hum stared. Hmmmm, I said to myself and put the glass in his empty dirty sink.

I pushed open the flimsy frame of the screen door like every old screen door that catches at the top and then lets go and slams into the wall stretching the spring across the hinge.

"Sorry," I said. But nobody had jumped.

"You care to sit a spell?" Rose asked from the next porch.

And for some reason I said, "No, ma'am, thank you." And thank you to Jimmy for the water. And I nodded to Layla but she wasn't paying me no mind and neither was Ambrosia who sat there rocking with such swings I thought the girl would rock right off the porch. Layla was my age or younger. Lord, I thought, Ambrosia must be six. What'd Layla do? Have her when she was thirteen?

That was when I turned and waved and almost stepped into the mess of the half-rotten raccoon I mentioned.

I stayed in a shelter for ladies in Memphis and strolled out past the three houses every now and then whenever we got bored of playing the used video game someone left with a bag of socks and canned goods one weekend with a note that said they hoped God would bless us all in the coming year. When Jimmy came around to asking me to stay he did it from his sofa right in front of Rose, Layla, and Ambrosia like they were all too tired from the heat to care. I didn't have anything but what I wore, so I climbed up on Jimmy's porch and sat on the lower end of his sofa colored like a green bean, and I started staring across the tracks waiting for the train like everybody else.

Somehow when a little donkey walked by the front porches and continued on around to the other side I wasn't surprised and nobody said anything about it. At the time I didn't even bother asking.

One
Month Free

It didn't take me much time to learn that Jimmy had four parts to his day. Working at the butcher shop. Sitting on the sofa. Loving my body. Working on his computer.

I had never used a computer and Jimmy eventually showed me all kinds of things, some good, some bad, some I can't think about. He got the computer for nearly nothing through a help-the-poor shebang. Then he set up a plan to get a month free from the Internet service, then switched to another month free from someone else, and so on, then back to the first company.

Watching Jimmy in the daytime you'd never know the kinds of things he found on that computer in the nighttime. I've always been able to sit for a long time and not get bored or get fidgety. So I was still enough for him to forget me while he sat with all the lights out, glowing in the blue like baby Jesus in the manger.

Jimmy in front of the computer screen was like me in

front of a magazine rack. I told him that once, but when he was watching the computer he hardly heard a thing.

He said the computer was how he was getting out. I didn't ask him what he was getting out of because some things you get out of but you don't have to move, like owing money. Other things I didn't want to think about at the time.

There were all sorts of educational programs. When I first moved in he was mostly looking at meat-processing sites. They'd give him ideas about how to be a better butcher. I couldn't hardly look at the stuff. All the details of animals strung up by their back feet or thrown into a crate by their legs in the case of chickens was better left to professionals, if you ask me. He agreed it took time to get a stomach for the work. And maybe not everyone can handle it. But if you can, it can become a favorite thing to do.

Well, let him have it. I'd find another job.

He claimed he could learn anything on the computer. Watching him, I believed it. But some things are best not known. I once saw him at the butcher counter in the store when he didn't know I was watching. I was proud of him. He was very professional-looking and crisp in his cutting and the way he ripped the white paper to wrap up the meat then stuck on the price tag all in one motion. It was like he protected people from knowing how the meat got there. But he watched it all, every detail, on the computer.

Later on when I told him Rose was likely gonna die he got on the computer and started finding all sorts of sites to buy coffins. Then he got the idea that between his strong stomach and the knowledge he could get at on the computer he might just preserve her himself. Or cremate her, which was ridiculous because he'd have to do it in the yard and there are always people walking down the tracks and train conductors with their faces hanging out the window staring at everything passing by since they don't have to steer. I said they were not likely to be happy with that. And he asked who They was. And I said the people that made the law, invented the Internet, wrote commercials, and prepared dead bodies for the ground.

He rolled his eyes and said that he had met plenty of Them in his time and They weren't any better at coming up with rules that made sense than anybody else. Didn't matter, I said, because if They can get you in trouble, that's all you need to know. He rolled his eyes again and didn't say anything either because he knew I was right or else because he thought you can't argue with a girl, which is not true.

But he liked a mystery and another idea came to him and he found an Internet site where he could train as a private detective. That made some sense except that you don't have a steady income so sometimes you might have no work at all and what are you gonna do then? But to tell the truth he also looked at being a spy and joining a foreign army and I didn't say anything because it made me start to understand what he meant by the computer being the way he was getting out. I'm sorry but that's just not the world I live in. Mine's about fifty feet by thirty feet. With an occasional walk to the bridge or to church. Luckily he was not one to just up and quit his day job.

When I sat over against the wall it didn't look like much. Just Jimmy glowing, moving his hand around slightly, clicking with his pointer finger. But what a world, what a world. I started to get scared for Jimmy. The problem was that if he was looking at coffin stores or at spy opportunities or international money schemes or church addresses, he looked the same—push and click, push and click, glowing like a streetlamp.

He had blankets hanging from the windows to keep anyone from looking in. And pretty soon he didn't want me looking in either and that's when I moved over with Rose, but by then somebody was growing inside me.

I already mentioned that he'd bring scraps from work, but he started thinking less and less about his butchering and more and more about his computer. I didn't like it. Butchering is blood and meat and you get real money. The computer is pictures and electricity and you can't eat anything on it. When he thought up a way to use Layla and her gift from God to make money he must have gotten very excited. He hadn't paid Layla much mind I know of, but after his idea came to him everybody wondered why he was suddenly so interested in Layla.

Ho-Bo.com. Lord Jesus help us.

THE RATTLESNAKE

If I'd been paying more attention I might have noticed that God sent a sign. But it wasn't me that noticed the thing. Actually it was Layla who noticed, but she didn't notice the snake. She noticed Ambrosia who noticed the snake.

We were waiting for the train to pass. Wind from the train passing by eases the heat. It passes so close you can understand the end of the world. Rose always sat like nothing changed. As I said, you can get used to anything. But me—I always feel the train shake my bones.

That was why after watching Ambrosia rock right through the train passing day after day, even I didn't take long to notice that she wasn't rocking while the train passed. We all leaned in to see what she was staring at under the train, and as I said, Layla was the first to see.

"It's a goddamned rattlesnake," she screamed, though the poor thing was all curled up on the track and its rattle was going like crazy and the sound of the train drowned it out like a chorus of angels might drown any leftover grumblings in the Kingdom.

Then that little thing shot out between the wheels of that train and God witnessed us jump when it sprang but the steel wheel caught it on the tail and it rolled about ten feet then lay there like it was dead trying to figure out what happened.

A thing wants to live. That much is sure. So once the train passed we all settled back to see what the snake would do. We didn't talk. Ambrosia was back to rocking the second that snake sprang out. It was like she was only interested in the coiled-up snake but once it straightened out it didn't exist anymore.

But just when she lost interest I got interested because the question was is the snake dead and who's walking over to find out.

Nobody had to go kick the snake, though, because before we could even start talking like grown-ups about what just happened the snake started to slither. But it didn't slither off into the woods. It slithered toward the chicken-wire fence and then tried to poke its head through one hole then another like it was deciding. Then it found a torn place in the fence and came on through and I know we all felt our hearts going weak but we wanted to see where it would go after all that.

Well, it went up under Layla's porch before anyone could say anything, and the thing was done. Now we had a snake living with us and not just one that might or might not be dangerous but one we had seen the rattle knocked off of. And one ready to risk dying if that's what it took to live.

"That snake ain't gonna be warning nobody now," Rose said.

I hadn't thought about that, everything happened so fast.

And then like she knew we all got suddenly nervous she said in a comforting tone, "I bet if Jesus sees that snake he'll stomp him inside out." I haven't mentioned that the donkey's name is Jesus.

In time I learned from Rose that a quiet snake is like a dark mystery inside your body. Some mysteries are okay like the sounds your stomach makes even when you aren't hungry or why you have periods. That's just the mystery of having insides instead of being angels, she'd say. But other things are bothersome such as lumps and the way you can sometimes feel like something is wrong even if you don't have a lump. Then you start thinking about dying even if you are young, and it's worse if you are young because if you live a long time you end up having a lot of worry to look forward to. I agreed. But then the strange thing is that after all the worrying over false alarms, in some ways it's better to know you are soon to die and from what than to think about how it might be, she'd say. She didn't learn that until the day she decided she would die soon. When she said that's how it feels I hadn't even been thinking about the snake. But I saw what she meant.

Think about it enough and every step off the porch and every comfortable crawling into bed turns into a new chance to be scared, like every walk down the tracks past strangers, or when you go to the pharmacy to buy Band-Aids and see old people with swollen legs and feet with their shoes loose and untied, waiting on medicines and you know they are fighting something even if they grin at you when you walk by. It ain't death. It's the idea of death.

Jesus Is Coming Soon

It hurts sometimes but it's worth the trouble it causes looking sort of white to some black folks and sort of black to some white. I've learned some things being this way but there've been days I wished I was all one or the other.

The one time I don't feel any color at all is when I go for a walk. Not toward the city but away from it to the north. Memphis drops right off into a few lots of junk then sticks. That's the direction I walk.

I started doing this not long after I moved in with Rose and when I walked out there I looked out into the sticks and the mud and thought. On one tree settled back from the road was a crooked white sign with red letters painted on it that said, "Jesus is coming soon." It looked like it'd been there a while so I wasn't sure what it meant by "soon." But the thought worried me some. For one thing, this was my first baby and I wanted to see what it looked like. The only child I'd spent any time around besides memories of myself was Ambrosia, but she was always either rocking looking at her little cardboard book or else she had lost her book again and she was rocking and screaming and pulling her hair. Layla went nuts sometimes looking for that book if Ambrosia was screaming. I could tell already that my baby wasn't gonna be a screamer. Not that it mattered.

The other thing that bothered me was the sign being stuck out there in the middle of a bunch of dead sticks with nothing around but a few junkyards and some shacks. Maybe if it wasn't crooked it would've helped. A message or a warning like that should have a better sign. I walked on out to it and then turned around and came back, but I couldn't decide if all the mess and weeds and stacks of rubber tires ought to have made me feel glad or worried about Him coming.

Anyway, Rose seemed pretty set on Him coming, though if He didn't come soon I was afraid she'd miss it all. Jimmy didn't really care much one way or another I guess but that didn't stop him from looking up all kinds of religious strangeness on the computer. You'd be amazed what some religions do. And I couldn't talk to Layla about it, first because she did more staring than talking like she was always thinking about something other than what you were talking about and second because she was busy with one of the bums she was always bringing in off the train track.

Which was one of the strangest things about her, all the friends she made out of whatever or whoever happened to be wandering along the tracks. Not that she asked them. She could just be walking around the yard or even just leave her door open in the springtime like it was a sign saying come on in. When she had Ambrosia she bled a lot and they took out her womb. That was the other thing. My womb grew into a watermelon-sized thing any passing stranger could see and I sometimes felt funny talking to her knowing she didn't have her womb anymore. Especially being so young. And the problem was that it was not like missing a leg or being bald where everyone can tell what you're missing so that you go ahead and get used to it. It was missing something important that nobody sees or knows about unless you tell them, and then you always have to decide, do you tell them or do you not?

And body parts aren't the only thing you can be missing. Other things that aren't body parts can be taken away. But you still have the same problem about whether you tell somebody or not. And then you don't know if they will still like you. If you are missing a leg a person can decide ahead of time whether they like people who are missing legs. But if you are missing a womb, or if one of those other things has been taken away, then they can't decide if they still like you until you are already in the middle of it. Meet a couple of people who decide they don't like you once they find out what's missing, and sometimes you just stop wanting to let people get to know you.

So if Jesus was coming soon I wasn't complaining, but He was sure to find a whole lot of folks who think a whole lot different than Him. The world's just not the same as it was back then from what I hear in church. But I wasn't worried about Him. In the meantime I kept tending Rose. She was good to me and I knew I'd miss her when she died and somehow I hoped my baby got here before she died so that at least the house wouldn't be empty. When somebody dies you don't want the house to be empty because it's too much at once. Even a cat can help if it's friendly and not the kind that disappears for days at a time, but a person is much better for this kind of thing.

And last, I wouldn't say this to just anyone but I used to think of Jesus as a white man, even though in the churches I went to he was painted as a black man but with hair that was more like a white man's or else pressed straight with hair softeners. When I think of Jesus coming it's hard for me to think about him being so white, and just as hard thinking about him using hair softeners. But once I learned to think of him like a donkey in some ways, which I knew was probably not right, it helped since thinking that way I could see him walking around saying, "All right, folks, it's time to go," instead of coming with some big flash of light. When I think of Jesus as being sort of like a donkey I'm not so bothered by that sign being crooked or stuck in the sticks and muck or painted with big red letters. A man white or black might mind that. A donkey would just walk by and not care the least. Even if it's wrong when I think of Jesus like a donkey, I can pray again.

The Donkey Named Jesus

But I have to say that it's not always easy having a real donkey around instead of just a painting or an idea. He mostly stays out back where he does his business. If the little bit of breeze we ever get comes off the tracks it's fine, but if it comes the other way it smells like a zoo. There's no latch on the gate in back and Jesus pushes through whenever he's hungry and eats weeds growing in the field nearby then always comes back. He can't pull the gate closed so Jimmy fixed up a rope from the gate into Rose's kitchen window so I could just pull on it and close the gate.

He's a little thing and he's old and has lots of gray in his muzzle. He never seems to mind if the train is passing by or if Ambrosia is screaming and during the summer when the windows are open if he stretches his neck he can just barely get his nose up to the window to sniff. There must've been something about the smell in Ambrosia's room because if he wasn't wandering around the back side you could just about bet you'd find him sniffing at Ambrosia's window, just standing there with his body still as a rock.

Ambrosia pays him almost no mind. Even if he comes near and sticks his nose by her hair she just rocks and turns the pages of her little book. If I was to come near her cheek she'd swat me like a bug without even looking at me. I can understand thinking of wind and rocks and bugs as things you just feel or push or swat. But she seems to think of people that way, like they are just things moving around and she doesn't want to be bothered. Jesus is more like a part of her body, like her own leg, which she might move if it started to ache or bother her.

The first time I saw Jesus nuzzling Ambrosia I worried that he was gonna bite her. I would never think that now that I know him. But at first what I thought was that Layla just didn't pay enough attention to her girl. Now I think she was jealous in a way that Jesus could nuzzle the girl without being pushed away and Layla couldn't. But I could never say that.

When the donkey turns away to nibble grass there's spit in Ambrosia's hair half the time. If it was my girl I'd wipe it off right away. But Layla just let it sit and dry while she looked out over the tracks sometimes sipping on lemonade. And Jesus clomped around the yard.

It's embarrassing to say anything about Jesus's maleness, which is very noticeable sometimes, even though he is a little donkey. But I couldn't help but giggle and Jimmy and Rose joined in with Rose sometimes saying, Lord have mercy, which was funny coming from her lips and knowing that she'd seen just about everything. But Layla just stared and sipped her lemonade without any joking to make sense of the thing. Like one rock staring at another rock. It's one thing to see everything and another thing to see too much.

This is to say I am just amazed sometimes at how two people can be so different as me and Layla, even though we are about the same age. It's like the difference between a full moon and no moon. I didn't say that to Layla. She might've taken it as a comment on her womb.

Trees

The trees were the first things I saw from a distance when I came up on Rose's lot. They all looked like Ys. There were leaves on the trees since it was still summer and the row looked like the part in Jimmy's hair. The power company had been the ones who cut the trees into Ys so they could keep their lines clear, which was probably important. But the trees were sick and gray and truth be told the leaves they made didn't give much shade. Which made you wonder if trees could ever be more important than power lines and who decides. Or even whether if a tree is gonna be cut into some unnatural shape it might be more respectful just to cut it down and plant some flowers or a shrub.

But once this baby started growing I started looking at things as being the world a child would live in. And as I thought about why they had to cut the trees into Ys for lines that were so high up I came across one likely reason for such, that maybe it's the Law, and at the very same time I saw clearly that the Ys would make a good place for a tree house.

In fact, a plank long enough could run through the Ys we had in the yard, and quite a little fort could be built.

When you are nineteen you don't think about forts, if you ever did, which I didn't except for a couple of times. Once was when I first heard the story of Robinson Crusoe. The other was when I had been sent to stay with an uncle for a while when my mother was sick and I rode with him on his business to pick up valuables that people left on the street for the garbage men. We always started in the rich neighborhoods early in the morning and it was amazing what people will throw out. Mattresses, barbecue grills, humidifiers, stereos, you name it.

So one day we were driving through the neighborhoods and he said, "There it is," which is what he said whenever we came to a load that would give us in one stop as much as we usually found in a whole day. It was in front of a pretty brick house, big enough for three or four families easy. There was all kinds of things—toys, boxes of clothes, books, a bed, pictures, and all the pieces for a fort including a plastic roof and a little door. It was like Christmas except that I never had a Christmas like that. So we loaded up the truck but we didn't have room for the fort and I would have cried except that I knew I was only staying there for a little while and could never take it back to Memphis anyway. But when we had loaded everything up and we were pulling away I saw this white woman staring out the window. And then before I even knew why I cried anyway.

All which is to say that when you are pregnant and you

start thinking about forts again, you can wonder why you ever stopped thinking about them. I mentioned this to Jimmy but he saw too much room for extra work, though one night he took a break from his searches on the computer to find a site about tree houses. Everything was on that computer. Everything. If I had had the nerve I'd have gotten him to show me pictures of childbirth, but some things just need to be gone through and not thought about so much, I think.

So something catches your eye like three trees lined up and cut into Ys. Then the Y reminds you of the question Why and the trees look half dead like a lot of other stuff. One thought leads to another thought not like train cars, which are connected so that you know why they follow each other, but like ants who, if the first ant walks zigzag, every other ant walks the exact same zigzag, even though they are not connected by anything you can see. Then before you know it somebody who would not be around except you stopped and asked for a glass of water starts to grow inside you and suddenly you're not thinking about why people like the power company ruin your trees but instead how the trees might look to a kid, other than Ambrosia. And that's what made me wonder what else I was missing.

But this kind of thing is hard to say. Saying it is not really like the thing you want to say. It's like a tree's shadow is like a tree and also is the thing most not like a tree. Everything I'm saying is shadows. But what's inside—Lord have mercy, Christ have mercy.

Layla's Gift from God

Not to go on about a thing, but sometimes at night when I was rubbing my hand over my belly I thought of Layla and Ambrosia alone on the other side of Jimmy's house, and I imagined crazy things. Like Ambrosia as a sponge inside Layla soaking up too much of one part of Layla so that she was robbed of that part and Ambrosia was so stuffed full of it she had no room for anything else. Say she took all the fear. Or the rage. Or something. I couldn't even think what one thing it might be that Layla was missing that seems all stuffed into little Ambrosia rocking back and forth. Maybe shame. After I thought of Ambrosia sucking up all the shame, say, I saw her being born feetfirst and grabbing onto Layla's womb and pulling it out with her.

I didn't know what Layla was like before she lost her womb but I'd never seen anything quite like her. She was not pretty but she had the roundest breasts and the roundest firm bottom I'd ever seen. And she had three dresses all made of thin material and hiding nothing of who she was and she never wore panties. But it wasn't like she was showing off. It was more like that was the way she was made so it was hard to fault her. I think making love to Layla would be like standing in the shade when it's hot.

So men who wandered down the tracks just came to her room and she gave of herself. In the time I knew her I counted eighty-seven bums that she made love to. In the beginning I'd hear her scream and I'd think she was being beat. But when I made Jimmy go check, even though he said she was fine, Layla was sore at me for a week. "I was just worried is all," I told her, and that was soon after I started staying with Jimmy so how could I have known what was what in her life? But that didn't matter. Even when I explained she wouldn't say why she was mad that I made Jimmy walk in. It felt like walking in on a doctor's examination or a priest taking confession I guess.

So I just started listening to her scream while bum after bum found a night's worth of relief from whatever it was that kept them walking the tracks. It never just sounded like screams. It sounded like she was screaming at someone. But who? Not the bum, I'd say. Who else was there to scream at? God?

And I mean any bum could find that night of relief with Layla. It didn't matter young or old, smelled bad or not, fat or bony. I'd never seen anything like it as I said. I saw men missing limbs follow her into her house. I saw men I knew were retarded, and they never just walked up to the door like the others but she had to call to them while they stood in the corner of the yard and they always looked bashful when they came out and wouldn't look at me. And I saw men who except for not shaving and being on the tracks could be insurance salesmen for all you'd know. But there was never more than one at a time. That was just the way it was. And I never knew anyone to fight. If a man was already there the others just walked on like they understood the rules.

I wondered if they knew she didn't have a womb, and I was pretty sure they didn't because Layla was never a talker even to people she knew like me and Rose, though for some people it's true that the people you talk most to are people you don't know, people at the bus station, for example. I was pretty sure Layla's bums just went in and did their business and left without a lot of talking. I don't know where their seed went. There's a lot I don't know. But I was born a very curious person. If I had stayed in school I'd have been a scientist.

Sometimes I wish Ambrosia could talk because she heard every one of the bums and what passed between them and her mama.

I'll say again I can't fault her and wouldn't want to. When she was alone down at the other end on her couch, staring out at nothing in particular, she seemed heavy, like even standing up was a chore and she was just too tired to do it. Even when she went to church she just sat there looking down, and when she went up for the bread and wine she never looked at the priest, never crossed herself, just walked back to her pew where she didn't kneel or close her eyes or do anything but stare at the floor. But when one of her bums came along it was the one time she seemed to know what to do, which was interesting to me because as calm as she was motioning for them to go on inside, I'd throw up I'd be so nervous. For them I thought Layla was like shade on a hot day. That's as good as I can say it.

The Tooth Fairy's Castle

A while back Ambrosia lost her first tooth. We were all sitting on the back porch and the train was roaring by interrupting talk about the best ribs we'd had in Memphis. When it passed there was usually a time before we started up again. But this time just before I was about to say something Layla looked down and said, "You lost your tooth." And sure enough Ambrosia had pulled out her loose tooth and it was sitting by her on the porch. She had just the slightest bit of blood on her lower lip.

I saw that Layla looked like she wanted to cry and I thought I understood. I hadn't seen her look like this before, but you never know what's gonna make you cry. Most kids get all excited when they lose a tooth but Ambrosia plucked it out like a piece of grit and set it off to one side.

Then Layla reached down and picked up the tooth and held it up. She said, "You want me to put it under your pillow for you?" and she said it like she was blaming somebody. Ambrosia of course kept rocking and Rose looked out over the tracks with a face that said, How long, Lord, how long?

Which made me think of a story that a woman from the government who used to visit my mother to make sure she took her infection drugs told me when I lost a tooth. It wasn't much of a kid's story I can see now and it scared me at the time. "There's not much to the tooth fairy," the lady told me. "She got nothing to do with the day and only works when it's dark and people don't see, don't guard what they think about.

"She doesn't talk. And for her, money is nothing more than a way to buy the bones of children. A tooth is a bone and her castle is made of these small bones that children lose to remind everyone that children grow old like everybody. The castle glimmers with a kind of bluish light over the surface of it. There are no windows. The sun shines silver in those parts. Never red. Never yellow.

"She is tiny. She is so tiny. And each step up to her front door is made of a single tooth. There are a thousand steps to keep away visitors, and twice as many inside, each one from a different child somewhere in the world.

"She lives alone in the daytime and she sits on her tiny throne at the top of all those teeth in her white lace and tiny white shoes and see-through wings, and she cries. She cries all day long, so much that her tears fall from her face down the smooth surface of children's bones and in summer they form a pool far below so that the whole castle is reflected. In the center of that liquid mirror is the tooth fairy.

"In the winter her tears form icicles and by the time the winter is deep it looks like a long white beard hanging from her high perch down to the smooth floor below.

"She has no one to ask her why she cries because the rule was written that she can only take the tooth of a sleeping child. She has long since had enough bones for her castle with endless empty rooms. So she uses them to build mountains. She has no questions, and she has no idea how happy the children are when they wake up and find the tooth gone and replaced with a coin. She only knows the way things have to be. She doesn't even know why she cries all the time. But I know."

That was it. I just stared at the lady while she went back to checking my mother's medicines and making sure she took them. Which made me wonder why somebody who would take a job doing that would tell a story like that to a kid. But since then I met enough people who do those kinds of jobs to learn that even things that look like kindness can wear on you like anything else if you don't get a break sometimes. That's part of what I thought about with the baby because it was just me, and Jimmy was part time at best. I hoped that being a mother made you change somehow so that you can do it all the time without needing a break, but I knew that didn't always happen. Of course it may be that she just thought it was a good story and didn't see that it sort of ruined the tooth fairy. Some people don't know how to tell a story and don't know when.

But when I thought of the story I thought of where Ambrosia's mind spends its days. I looked at Layla. She sat there for the longest time looking at that tooth like she was deciding whether or not to eat it. Ambrosia wouldn't have noticed and wouldn't have minded if she did notice. She just rocked and turned the pages of her cardboard book.

The Closed World

While Rose worked on whether or not she was gonna die I worked on a jigsaw puzzle of Paris, France. A thousand and one pieces laid out on the card table in Rose's room. She felt better when I was near.

I always liked jigsaw puzzles. I used to have a girlfriend Mattie who said, What's the use of putting all the pieces together if you already have the picture on the front? I never knew what to answer her. Then she would ask me what I was gonna do when I finished? Just stand there and look at it? Ask somebody else to look at it? No, I'd say, maybe I'll put it on cardboard and hang it up on the wall like I read about in a hobby magazine. And she'd say, Why? You didn't paint it. All you did was put the pieces together somebody else had cut out. And for a while I wouldn't have so much fun putting a puzzle together. Then I'd start again. And what I figured out was a few things. First, I liked finishing a thing. Second, if you pick a good puzzle you see a lot more about the picture by watching it form and by picking pieces with the right colors.

Anyway, I was working on Paris, France. I had the four edges finished, which is always the easiest part, and I was sorting the pieces by color looking at the picture on the front.

Rose said, "Yslea?"

"Yes, ma'am," I said with my tongue between my lips. I was concentrating on blue.

"What you making for dinner tonight?"

It seemed the less she ate the more she was interested in food. "Squash and fried okra."

"Squash and fried okra," she said. And seemed to think it over. "You know how many meals I've eaten? No matter, I never get tired of fried okra."

I found which blue pieces went next and had some luck finally placing their shapes into their opposites.

She lifted up her hand with her palm to heaven and the flesh just hung off her arm like a loose sleeve. "I hope Jimmy takes care of you and that baby."

I didn't say anything. I hadn't even decided if I wanted him to. And after seeing what all he found on that computer—it was just too much. Why would I want my baby around that? And it wasn't just the things he found on the computer. Those things are part of the world and you can't get away from the world because where would you go? But it was the way he liked to see those things so much and liked to be by himself when he looked. You can't have a family if you can't even walk into the room whenever you want, especially if you only have a couple of rooms. But I didn't go on about this to Rose.

"Anyway," she said, like she understood, even though I didn't say it, "you can stay here as long as you want after I'm dead. I won't have much use for the house then."

I didn't know what to say to her. Was she giving me the house? I wondered. I didn't think to ask if it was hers in the first place because that seemed rude. But I thought about four walls of my own even if it only had three rooms and a bathroom. When somebody who's lucky to own a dress and a pair of shoes finds out all of a sudden they might be able to own a house, they can't be blamed if they act strange. I put down my puzzle piece and took the yellow dress she wanted to be buried in out of the closet. She only moved her eyes to look at it. Then she looked away.

Why did I pull out that dress? I think to tell her not to worry after she was dead because I would take care of her, which was what I could give.

But her eyes told me something like "I'm not dead yet."

And I felt bad. Because it was true that I felt happy about the house, even though it meant she had to die. Sometimes a thing can go from good to bad in no time. But I am lucky that, even though sometimes when my brain chatters to me it makes it hard to concentrate on sermons, sometimes when it chatters to me it gives me good advice and tells me when to just be quiet and see if things pass. That's what it did. The other thing I am lucky about is that instead of being stuck on the inside of my life all the time, which is what can happen when you feel a lot, I usually seem to be watching myself do things, like I'm sitting in the corner nodding yes or shaking my head no.

I put the dress back and sat down again. My worry was that now anytime I was kind to her it might seem like I wanted her house. I didn't know what to do, so I waited. Everything had suddenly gotten so strange. But she knew what to do. "Yslea," she said.

"Ma'am?"

"You might get Jimmy to paint the walls a color the baby'll like."

"Yes, ma'am."

And then just to make sure everything was clear she said, "But not 'til I'm dead. Paint fumes make me cough."

I wanted to laugh but didn't know if I could. So I looked over at her.

She was grinning so I laughed, and part of why I was laughing was that Rose always knew what to do and I wanted to be like that for my baby, with plenty of room to take any of my child's mistakes and just hide them away inside myself so she can keep starting over until she gets it right. Which was a strange thing because until I thought that thought to myself I didn't know I thought my baby was a girl.

"Yes, ma'am. Thank you."

Things beneath the Grate

But that did make me start thinking about the house in a new way because I started thinking about the baby living in it for a long time instead of just thinking about me living in it for a bit. Even though my baby was still little I felt enough of her inside me that I started thinking more about what it would be like for her to be in my arms, about where she might sleep, about the locks on the doors and about the heat of summer and the cold of winter. People in Memphis are better at hot than they are at cold so once I started thinking about this my main worry about Rose's house was the heater, which Rose said was gonna be a problem that winter since it sometimes didn't come on the winter before. I don't like to be cold and I sure didn't want to be cold and pregnant. Who knows what cold does to an unborn baby? I thought. And I thought when my baby finally was born I just wanted not to worry about locks and heat and cold. I wanted not to worry about food.

Once I started thinking about it, though, it didn't take

long before I realized the problem might not be as big as I thought at first. I decided not worry about a problem that was not a problem yet. The ducts and vents and all were there. And these days machines like heaters work much better than in the old days.

But while I stood there mulling the house in general I stared down into the grate over the dark duct that snaked up to the middle of the house. My toes were on the edge and I looked down past my belly where my baby was growing and for the first time in a long time I thought about some of the things that used to scare me and thrill me and make me feel safer when I was a girl and for a minute or so I let it all just be one thought and suddenly I was both happy and sad that I was not a little girl anymore. And I wanted to cry, which was happening more and more often.

I kept looking down trying to work the thoughts all the way to the end. It was a kind of tunnel down there, with its own wind, where the house breathed. When I was a kid I stared and stared down through our grate, even though the adults stepping over me told me to get on up off that floor, girl. But there was a whole history of dropped things down there—candy wrappers, Band-Aids, bits of cereal, dust. But what I always saw as a kid about the things beneath the grate was that they were so different down there matted in the dark tunnel. They were the kinds of things you would poke at with a stick like a bug or dead thing you didn't want to touch, even something you would touch while it was new and fresh. Which makes sense since even a person who you might have hugged a thousand times can be like that when they are down in a coffin and it's all of a sudden hard to touch them. It's not just because you don't want to smudge the makeup they spent so much time putting on so that it's not so sad to look at dead people. And it's not just that you worry over not knowing whether their skin will feel room temperature or colder than that and you'll think it's gross and feel bad because that was the thought you had the very last time you touched them. It's because they used to be there and now they aren't and even if you're grateful to the dead body for being who you loved so long, you can't get to what changed. Everything is there in the box that was there before your friend or mama died. The only thing missing is your friend or mama. You wouldn't hug a person who didn't want to be touched or read even a good friend's diary without permission, and it's sort of like that. With a dead person, there's no one left to give permission. Something is hard about that touch.

I couldn't spend too much time thinking about that sort of thing, though. I never used to think this way. Maybe that is what a baby will do to you, make you think hard over the meaning of the smallest thing, since a baby is the smallest thing for a while. I was growing up. The way I knew I was growing up was that when I stared down through Rose's grate I also wondered why it was different down there instead of just feeling that it was different. I was getting better and better at wondering why instead of just feeling. Then I realized I'd been standing there a long time fretting over something that may be nothing and thinking about these other things, and I saw what I was doing and I stepped back. Every now and then everything seemed so strange to me, even little things like the duct and the heater, and I could only guess that part of the reason was having a baby growing inside me.

So even though I tried to make myself not think about problems that weren't problems yet, like the heater, I still mentioned it to Jimmy. He said don't worry. By the time winter got cold he'd have enough money to take care of a heater and anything else that came up. He was the kind who could have gone to college except that something, some invisible choke collar, kept him at his butcher job living right where he was born. I never knew much about what happened to his parents and his half-sister and he was living proof that if you stay in the same place long enough you're bound to get ahead somehow because he owned his house free and clear. But it was never enough for Jimmy. There was always something more than a roof, a job, a car, and even a computer to work on and search for things and do calculations and all. Jimmy was a big thinker, not a big actor. And that was Jimmy's problem. If he could have ever gotten his thinking and his acting in the same room he could have been running the meat counter instead of working for someone who ran it.

But when Jimmy talked about money he was handsome. It's good to see a man really want something. It's not that I don't agree with the priests about money and heaven. But it's not having money that keeps the heater from working. It's not having money that makes us glad even to have squash and okra. It's not having money that makes a lot of things hard. But I didn't ask about where he planned to get the money for the heater. I didn't like what Jimmy was up to.

Ho-Bo.com

So this was Jimmy's idea. I told him it was evil to his face and he just grinned, which was why I wasn't sure I'd ever want to move in with him again, especially once the baby was born.

"It's just money, baby," he told me. "It's just money."

He was good with money. He saved most of what he made at the butcher shop and he didn't drink and got meat for a fine price, even if some of it was sort of grayish. So it wasn't that he was evil. Just his idea.

He was always looking for a way to make some money. For a while he tried to get Layla to charge a little something to the bums who came in off the train tracks. He even said he might set up a little money bench outside the door. He tried it once when she wasn't looking. But when he went inside Jesus came around the corner and in the process of nibbling on the sandwich Jimmy had left there he knocked over the bench. Layla heard the ruckus and came out and told Jimmy none of this was his business and he could just take his bench back inside.

Then he found out you could buy these little cameras that plug into your computer. He said he could set up just one little camera in the corner of her room where nobody could see it and he could put her on the computer.

It didn't take any time for her to say no. But then he came back with some arguments. It wouldn't cost the bums a dime. She would become famous. She let this stop her for just a second. But then she shot another no back at him. Then he said he'd split the money sixty-forty with her. "What money?" she asked. And he told her it was easy to charge people's credit cards and all they wanted to do was watch. He had it all figured out and all she had to do was to keep doing what she was doing and he'd take care of the rest.

So if ever Layla lost her soul I'd guess that was when it was. I didn't know what all passed between her and the bums but it always seemed kind of sad to me and I figured they were lonely. But this turned it into something else.

And what made it worse was how Jimmy set everything up like it was just putting air in a tire or taping cardboard over a cracked window. He drilled holes in his wall and her wall that were about two feet apart and leaning toward each other. Then he ran his camera cord through the holes and wrapped the cord in plastic wrap, which I told him was ridiculous because when it rained the water would still get inside and the plastic would fall off. But he wrapped it with nearly a whole box of plastic wrap and when I said he'd have to go get another box because that was all I had, he said fine, with all the money he was gonna make, it was worth it.

At first I didn't see how it worked. But then he showed me one day. Up on the top line on his computer he typed, "Ho-Bo.com." Then came a few pictures of Layla sitting on the porch or standing by the chicken-wire fence leaning against the tree, which she never did I pointed out, or looking out over the tracks. The biggest picture was of her face and she looked a little bit mad, and I knew she had been mad because I had watched Jimmy take it. He kept asking her to look like she was pouting and she said she was pouting, but he said sexy pouting and she said he was ridiculous, which I agreed with and she walked away, so he had to make do with what he had.

There were a few movies to pick from and he clicked on one and there was a movie of Layla and one of her bums who I recognized there on the bed doing it. It was evil enough that the bum didn't get to have a say in whether or not his business was all over the computer for everyone to see, and all I could say was I sure hoped the bum never figured out how to get on the computer because he wouldn't be happy and Jimmy wasn't all that big and not much of a fighting type. But what made it even more evil was seeing Ambrosia down on the floor by the bed rocking and flipping through her cardboard book.

When I saw that I had to scream at him under my breath so that Rose wouldn't hear me. "Jimmy, that is the most god-awful thing I have ever seen anybody do." And then I tried to find the most hurtful thing I could say. "I'm ashamed," I said, "to have you as the daddy of my baby."

I could tell this stung him all the way down to his center because he just turned back to his computer screen and clicked to some other place on the web and started looking at whatever it was. The China Wall I think, which he seemed to like to look at. It hurt me too to say it but it was worth it because it was the only thing I could find to say that was big enough to make the point.

I didn't dare tell Rose. You can't help but wonder whether old people might not understand modern evil since it takes so much technology to make it happen, and when it does happen it's not like one man fighting another man with a club or a rock but like dropping a bomb on a whole city. These days they may even have one big enough to drop on the whole world. Same with Jimmy's computer. Sneaking a peak doesn't surprise anybody even if it can make you mad. But the computer lets you turn sneaking a peak into a whole business and from the way Jimmy described it you could be by the China Wall and see that poor bum who thought he was just having himself a nice little night.

I started watching Layla to see if there was any change. Since she never talked much anyway and just stared out to the tracks thinking whatever it was she thought, it was hard to pick up any changes. But then one day she stepped out on the porch in a new dress.

"That's a nice-looking dress," Jimmy told her.

She didn't answer or even look at him and I sat over on

my sofa not having any part of it. I wanted no part.

With old people it's hard to tell if they're too old to understand new kinds of sin or if it's that they're too tired to judge or if it's something they remember about themselves, but even though Rose would tell me if I asked, "I'm thinking about big things child, big things," I did not hear her say a word against Layla. But I worried that evil might seep through the walls. And that was the difference between me and Rose—I was having a baby and had to think about things like that.

Bathroom without a Heater

Even when fall days are warm, the nights make the bathroom the coldest place in a house. Every other place in the house is made of wood, which will soak up water until it rots. But the bathroom is made to not care about water. The ceramic of the toilet, the tub and the sink couldn't care less about water being on it. And in the late fall the hot weather just drops off and once the bathroom gets cold it stays cold until spring. Just to walk in and brush your teeth hurts your feet. And to sit on the cold toilet makes you gasp and makes it hard to go.

They say we're made of sixty or seventy percent water, which is part of why I think about the bathroom the way I do. When you heat water on the stove and put it into the tub to make a warm bath it's like you're building a place to be happy in, a place that doesn't care what you're made of. And you cross your legs and put your arms by your sides to get them under the warm water. Then your head bobs up and down and your face feels the cold then the warm then the cold. Then you get pregnant and there's just no keeping everything under the warm water.

But as it is, everybody has to get out and then you're not just cold but you're wet and cold, which makes you wonder whether it was worth it. It was hard enough for me, being young. But if I was Rose with all her stiff joints I'd wake up dreading all the cold I had to put up with just to have a clean body.

And that was why I wasn't surprised at the snake when Layla came running out onto the porch screaming in her see-through nightgown with Ambrosia under one arm screaming even louder and she said the rattleless rattlesnake was in her bed. Because what would you do if you had a choice between sleeping under the house and crawling up to sleep in a warm bed?

But she screamed until Jimmy finally agreed to go in and check just to make her be quiet, even though he was probably more scared of snakes than me and Layla put together. So he got his bat and went on in to see.

We waited for noise but nothing came and I wondered if Jimmy was just standing right inside the door long enough for us to think he was looking for the snake so he could get out of there quick without actually finding the snake. But pretty soon he came out with a grin on his face.

"I killed your snake, Layla."

And he held something behind his back but I knew it wasn't a snake because Jimmy wouldn't touch a snake even if it meant two hundred more men would sign up to his web site. But he pulled his hand around real quick and threw a long black thing toward Layla so that even I was shocked. And she screamed and dropped Ambrosia and covered her face.

Ambrosia hit the porch and in a second was sitting up rocking, quiet. She was just the opposite of most kids who'd be quiet under their mama's arm and scream if they were dropped. She was opposite in all kinds of ways and didn't even seem to mind that the black thing had dropped on her leg.

"It's just an old umbrella slipcase stuffed with dirty socks. One of your friends is gonna be missing his socks it looks like."

But Layla was so mad I thought she'd pop and she came over to Jimmy and started hitting and scratching so that he had to go inside his house and lock the door to let her calm down. And she didn't calm down right away so that I almost wondered if we'd have to call the police because what Jimmy did was childish, but after a while it was pretty clear she was raging about more than Jimmy's snake joke. He should have thought about that before he pulled his little stunt, though, because Layla was like a water balloon when it came to rage and a tiny prick didn't lead to the slow leak you'd expect with a small hole but the whole thing just popped at once.

Jimmy told me later she put masking tape all over the little camera eye and he had to increase her cut to fifty-fifty before she would take it off again. But I told him I didn't want to hear about any of that. I wanted no part.

Still, an idea's an idea and we all started looking carefully in our bedsheets before crawling in. And I couldn't keep my eyes closed in the bathtub anymore for fear the snake would find its way into the warmth. A creature knows what it wants, what it needs.

Roots Grow in Winter

They say roots grow in winter. I don't know how they know, but then I don't know how they know most things. If it's true I can understand it. Cold makes you stay put, which I guess is important for root growing. That was how I needed to think about winter while the baby grew. That was why I was happy about Rose wanting me to stay. Between Rose and Jimmy I was starting to feel this was my home. I didn't feel much about Layla. And I felt something but couldn't quite say what it was for Ambrosia. Down there just two houses away where they lived was so much sex and strangeness that it was different than any life I'd known.

But I was learning about some kinds of happiness and some kinds of hurt that change with the season. I did the laundry as part of why Rose let me stay without paying anything. Once a week I put together all our clothes, which were almost all worn-out flowered dresses and underwear, and I washed them in the metal tub. When it was warm and the water was warm and I knew the sun would dry the clothes with the wind and make the cloth feel thicker, I was happy. But in winter, even though I wouldn't call it pain, it still hurts somehow to do the washing. The clothes never seem as clean and if it's freezing you have to hang them up inside and they dry without smelling like wind. If it's not freezing you can still hang them outside, but your hands get stiff and it's harder to squeeze the clothespins and your knuckles always look more wrinkled after washing in the winter.

Of course I did more to earn my keep, like trying to figure out a way to cook beans so they'd taste different, cleaning up, helping Rose take a bath, which took a lot of time heating up the water since she liked it hot, and making sure she didn't break a bone. And all that was left was time to sit for a minute with my hand on my belly wondering why my baby was so still and quiet. In the summer we did everything in sunlight and warmth so it felt different. My walks were happier in the summer too, so except for the fact that it was the only way to get to spring, I did not like the winter.

But other things grow in winter besides roots. Since it's cold people stay inside and get ideas. People can see what you're doing in the summer and they can see more of you. It was being inside all the time that let Jimmy get his ideas.

And when it was cold Rose complained more about not being able to feel her feet, so her feet were just not made for true winter. They say a tree dies from its roots up. I wondered if roots are just as likely to die in winter as grow.

I never have understood people who live up North where it's always cold. How can anyone like being cold? But I guess some animals do. Polar bears and such. I'm the kind that when it rains hard I feel sorry for the roof and if an old bike sits in someone's yard and rusts I feel sorry for the bike too. But then I think about roots. And in the worst time I can think of, being buried under the freezing-cold earth, that's the time they grow. All I can think about is being dead when I think of cold earth.

I guess that's how I should've thought about Layla since I didn't understand what she needed much more than I understood how a root can need the cold. I just couldn't imagine needing what she seemed to need to live. Sex and church. She was how I got to the Catholic Church in the first place. One Sunday I was gonna go on a walk and I saw Layla already out walking the opposite direction from what I usually walk so I followed her and that's where we ended up. She always stared at the floor a long time after she took communion, praying probably. I didn't sit with her but I watched her from the back where I sat. I knew she knew when I was at church and it seemed strange that she didn't say hello and just sat there even when the priest said to pass the peace, which I also didn't like much because even if I was having a bad day I had to smile and say peace over and over. But I think Layla still might have felt better at church with me there, even if she couldn't say so. Sometimes you can't ask for what you really want, but if it comes your way you're glad it did. Even though we were not close and didn't even talk very much I was glad she was there also. Otherwise the only person I would have known would have been Jesus, and not that that's not enough, but sometimes you like to see a person instead of just feeling them there.

But all those bums going in and out. And after a while it wasn't just bums. I just don't know was all I had to say about it.

Raccoon by the Railroad Tracks

The raccoon I almost stepped in the first day took its time rotting. It was sprawled stomach down, four paws out. As the insides were taken away by whatever small creatures tend to that sort of work, the gray-striped pelt deflated and hairs blew away along with the dust. And eventually the creature's skeleton all bleached by the sun lay perfectly placed along the tracks with its ribs and spine reminding me of the orderly laying of tracks. Or maybe it was the other way around. In any case, I'd been watching it for a time.

I finished my jigsaw puzzle and let it sit there for a while. Then I asked Jimmy to buy some glue at the grocery where his butcher counter is and I mounted the puzzle like they did in the hobby magazine. I hung it up on Rose's wall and it was often that I looked in and saw her eyes looking over toward Paris, France, where she'd never been. So I was glad I finished the puzzle and didn't let old doubts keep me from doing my work.

But I got restless and wanted a new project. And that's when one day I went outside and got down on my knees, which was hard to do because my belly had gotten so big, to look more closely at the fine bones washed by rain and dried by the sun still resembling in their order the idea God must have had when He thought up the raccoon. The paws were made of many pieces including the curve of nails on each toe that made me think of raccoons hunched like old ladies, one paw lifted, turning their head toward the light.

Its bones were so orderly that I knew the work of lifting away its flesh was done by insects. Birds would have pulled the bones all here and there. The blackbirds on the telephone wire.

Next time I took my walk out to the sign of the end times I thought about the raccoon, nearly perfect, lying there next to the tracks. And that was when I decided it would be my next jigsaw puzzle. I figured the rain and the sun had done enough to kill whatever might still be living on the bones. The idea made me so excited that I could hardly wait to get back but I made myself walk on out to the sign because when I start something I am the kind of person who likes to finish it even if something else more interesting comes along. I haven't proven it yet but I have this idea that if I finish things it's good practice for when something comes along that is hard to finish but needs finishing anyway. I do it with the laundry, cleaning the house, puzzles, you name it. I will always do it with my baby too. You can't get half-way through being a mama and just decide to stop. Or you shouldn't anyway, even though I made it through so I guess it can be done. But I won't be that kind of mama.

When I got back I took the box with the picture of Paris and put the bones in it, careful not to break anything, one by one, making sure not even the tiniest foot bone was lost in the gravel between the ties. Then I took it in and put it on my card table and sat down to think about how to go about it. And that was when I started thinking. I mean really trying to think about things. For a long time I thought you had to be in school to think. And that the way you knew you'd thought something was that they gave you a certificate at the end to frame and hang on your wall. Rose didn't have one and neither did I. I knew I could still get one if I really wanted.

But this was when I started to think that that was not how you think, or at least that you don't have to have the certificate. Because I looked over to Rose and watched her old chest rise and fall like it had done since she first opened her baby-mouth and let out that first scream. Then I looked into the box of jumbled raccoon bones. Then I looked at my belly where the still one was forming. And I swear I felt a thought. Not one that they had already premade. A real thought, the kind that comes crusted over in earth so that you have to wash it and work it and polish it to see the real colors and strangenesses in it.

All of sudden I knew something of why Rose said she was thinking of a big thing but she wouldn't tell me what it was, though I suspect it had something to do with dying, which is a thought that probably feels a lot different when it's close than when it's far away. It takes time to say or know what to say when you're thinking a big thing. And some real things just aren't gonna be said.

But this thought I felt didn't say right off whether it would let itself be said or not. It was more like a man in a dark coat who comes up to your fence and stands there. A white man. And no one is quite sure what to make of the situation.

We are made up of pieces but somehow we feel whole. That much I could start with. So I took the bones from the box one by one and I placed them on the table. But this puzzle didn't start with the border. It started in the center with the spine. And there wasn't any picture except my memory. It made me wish I'd paid even more attention. But I had paid enough to get started.

I was gonna build a certificate of my own out of the bones of the dead raccoon that would be proof to myself that I had felt a real thought all my own. I would mount it on a fine board.

And somehow I knew that this was the first time ever that such a certificate was gonna be made, which by itself is something worth thinking about, the idea that in all the world and all the history of the world nobody ever did exactly this thing, mounting the bones of a raccoon to make a certificate. I was doing something new that felt old. And that is how I learned with just a few more steps in the thought that even if it had been done by somebody before, which I knew it had not, it had never been done by me, which meant that it was still something that had never been done before in the history of the world. Of course like those ants I mentioned the next thought came that everything in a life is like that in a way and every life is like that in a way. And that is the amazing thing about ideas sneaking up on you because nothing in the world changes, but because of the idea that came from who knows where, everything in the world changes, so that even little things seem like they might become special paid attention to enough. I was suddenly very happy and I thought about church and about how Robinson Crusoe used to make lists.

Worlds, Whole Worlds behind Chicken-Wire Fence

This got me to thinking of parts and wholes. A lot of my day was spent sorting parts into wholes while I watched Rose die of something. That was the secret to the jigsaw puzzle of course. Working to make a whole picture out of pieces. Finishing a thing.

Rose had roused and was staring at Paris so I asked her, "How long've you lived here?"

"A long time, child. A long time." She sighed and then made me to understand. "Lord, Lord, a long, long time."

She was not given to long speeches unlike my own brain, which always takes advantage of the long silences such as those of waiting for an old woman to die and a baby to be born. Except when I'm looking for a jigsaw piece my brain talks to me like the world will end tomorrow and it better say everything it's got to say and more today. Then the next day the same.

When Rose did talk it was all of a piece and felt right at home in the house. But for a woman who reminded me of a living stump grown up right in the yard, as much a part of the earth as the earth itself, she sure talked in vagaries. Time was long but no particular length. Ideas were big but no particular size.

I learned that she had a common-law husband back years ago who died by having his face rot off from cancer from smoking and chewing little pieces of tar. But I had to learn the details from Jimmy and how he got them from Rose I don't know. That's the advantage of growing up in one place instead of moving around, you know all sorts of things about people that you don't even know how you learned or who told you. Everyone just slowly starts knowing the same things.

But then one day I had the raccoon bones spread all over the table and I was having fits over not being able to tell one foot bone from another and Rose sat up and said, "I saw Rufus clear as sunshine."

She seemed so taken with what she had seen that I asked, "Who is Rufus?" even though I was concentrating.

She said, "And his face was all better." So I knew it was her common-law husband. "All better," she said, "except for one eye, which was missing for some reason. But oh my, even that made him look handsome, strong, like someone who's been through what scares everybody else and just calmly looks around the world knowing that he is brave and full of knowledge. Lord bless me, I didn't know how much I missed him. I have wanted heaven. I have tasted the gift of heaven. My one-eyed cocky Rufus with a grin and a goatee."

Jesus happened to be sticking his nose through the open window right then. I sat among the dry bones listening to Rose's version of heaven and I knew there was some sort of grace settling over our homes, which I had heard preached but, like the idea that came to me, had to dawn and dawn and dawn again. I felt that soon I would see a miracle if indeed I had not already seen one or thought one.

I looked at Jesus. "Was Jesus here before you were?"

"No," she said, almost singing the o. "He wasn't here. He was on the other side of the fence. It wasn't until Rufus's face began to rot off that he nosed his way into the yard. And he would stick his face right into the window and raise his nose up into the air of the bedroom and sniff and the stench was high. Oh Lord Jesus, the lower half of Rufus's face was plumb gone and you could see his teeth and his nasty tongue hanging down, and he wiped saliva all day with a rag. I reckon that donkey must be over twenty years old."

"He seems taken with Ambrosia now."

"Yes. Yes. He smells need. He smells when things are gone wrong. And he lets evil float into his nostrils and I don't know what he does with it from there."

"Well, he's lived a long time."

"I expect." Since she was sitting up she could see over to my card table. "What you working on there?"

"A raccoon."

"It didn't come in that box?"

"No, ma'am."

"A raccoon," she said. And she lay down and went back to sleep.

Bare Sticks Bridge

At my church they are pretty good at doing Christmas and the first Christmas I had knowing there was a baby in me was special. The baby made that Christmas feel so different that even if I couldn't understand how Jesus is God at least I could understand Mary, which felt like a start. Even so, not to criticize but that Catholic Church sure doesn't let you enjoy Christmas long before they start planning Lent with all the crosses covered in black veils, which made me think of dying and of the fact that I was not married. After that I could hardly wait for Easter when they'd take off the veils and everything would be swallowed up in spring. It was the whole thought of getting to spring that made me walk farther when I went on walks to keep my blood flowing for my baby.

That was why I started the habit of walking out past the sign of the end times all the way to the bridge crossing the gully of bare sticks. Once winter drags on for a while people start keeping an eye out for buds and green things even when there is still a good stretch of cold left. But the bare sticks beneath the bridge are bare in winter and in spring they will still be bare. Along the gully they lie like there was once a flood that knocked them down in a line and then dried up. The others stick straight up with skinny trunks and no leaves, like they grew fast but the ground gave out on them and the nourishment was gone so that just as their tops peeked up over the bridge they died.

It's easy sometimes to forget how hard the world is, but it will remind you. Like the bridge. Most often my walks were nice and I liked the smell of the air. When I started walking out to the sign of end times and on past, by the time I got to the bridge I'd feel younger than I'd felt since I'd started growing a baby, feeling like I was twelve. So finally feeling all this one day I decided to follow a little path I'd noticed leading down through the bare sticks into the gully with another path shooting off underneath the bridge, just like a curious girl would.

There was a dark damp smell like the underside of a stone or a leaky church basement. There were rows of white fungus and those brown bugs that have thin shells and legs like eyelashes that you find in moist dark places. However much the bare sticks made the whole area around the bridge seem like nobody ever came, all the cans and bottles under the bridge told a different story.

Where the ground leveled out up near where the bridge grew out of the earth was a pink blanket and a nasty-looking backpack, which had to once be a child's with its Snow

White and the Seven Dwarves picture on the back. I looked around to see who was sleeping there but there was nobody to be seen. Which was worse in a way than seeing somebody.

Then the thought came to my mind that that rattlesnake had to come from somewhere, and wherever that was there might be more. All of a sudden I didn't feel twelve. I felt a pregnant nineteen and I had started to get on out from under that bridge when I heard a scratching noise like an animal from up in the crevice between the earth and the bridge.

"Give us some of that," came the short nasty little grunt from the crevice.

Then I saw him, the filthiest man I'd ever seen with his brown hair all matted and his beard twisted like it was full of sticks and he was wearing a nasty torn T-shirt that said Swarthmore College and had a wet spot on it, and wherever Swarthmore College is I felt pretty sure he hadn't gone there.

"Give us some of that," he said again. He was crouched down on his haunches in that small space and he waddled forward like a duck. "Give us some of that."

"Some of what?"

"Give us some of that," he grunted again before I barely got my words out.

I didn't know what that white man was gonna do but I got on out of there. The dirt was loose and I slipped and got dirty but I got out of there. He could see I was pregnant but some people you can't figure. You just got to run.

I heard him back there shuffling around like a rat and after I got up on the street I saw his nasty head peek up over the bridge and he said one last time, "Give us some that." Then he sort of laughed with a "heh heh" and darted his eyes around crazy like the daylight scared him and he went back under his bridge.

So from then on I knew we had a troll of our own, which was one of those things I learned is interesting when it is just a story but not when it is real. I didn't even want to know what was in that Snow White backpack or what he did all night up under that bridge.

That night as I was thinking about all this I wondered if Layla had ever had the Troll. And it made me feel very strange toward Layla and strange toward what all she must remember about her life.

The Black Easy Chair

First I noticed Layla in that new dress. Then I noticed that sometimes when Jimmy brought me and Rose some meat it wasn't gray. But I knew Jimmy was making some money when I came home from my walk and saw the black easy chair on Jimmy's porch instead of his tilted sofa.

The train was going by and it must have been a mile long so all I could do was stand there and wait for it to pass so Jimmy could explain about the chair. He had a glass of iced tea in his hand and while he sat there you could see he was trying not to grin.

That black easy chair had been something Jimmy had talked about for as long as I had been there. It had been down at Potter's Pawn Shop, which specialized in handguns and appliances and such, and every clear morning old Potter would drag that chair out front of his shop to get his customers' attention, and every evening he'd drag it back inside with the help of his otherwise useless boy, Dimitri.

Dimitri, who was probably thirty years old, sat behind

a glass window and anytime you walked into the pawnshop just to browse he'd stare at you like you were about to steal something and you were doing it naked with shoes on. He'd open his cash register and close it, then open it and close it like he wanted to remind you that he had a drawer full of money and you didn't. And he'd do it from behind the box he sat in with bulletproof glass thick as a door so that even if you wanted to get to him you couldn't unless he let you.

I had been to the pawnshop with Jimmy so I knew. He used to look at that chair, rub his hand along the back and then sit in it until Dimitri said, "Are you planning on buying that chair?" meaning don't sit in it unless you have some money to buy with. But it was covered in leather and there was no way for Jimmy to afford it. So instead of buying it he thought about it like you'd think of a vacation where you go to another state and stay in a hotel, or else like a wedding where they serve champagne. And he'd talk about it on the way home like the chair was part of what he meant when he said, "This is my way out."

Not that it was anything to my eyes but a black chair. It even had some of those cracks a chair gets when you sit in it too long or sweat.

Still, I hated Dimitri for making Jimmy feel like that back then, and I hated him even more because there was a hobby section of the pawnshop where they had X-Acto knives, paint sets, and a telescope. I have always thought that if I had paints and X-Acto knives I could make my own jigsaw puzzles. But I especially liked that telescope because, even though it only makes the moon a little bit bigger, it is one of the things that makes you feel closer. Not closer to the moon so much. Just closer.

But when Dimitri was working—not his dad, since Potter was too drunk and kind and used to being black in the South to work without seeming courteous, though he especially didn't trust black people, I know, and he loved whites to come to his store, which they did to buy black memorabilia for their living rooms. As I was saying, when Dimitri was working, there wasn't any sitting around dreaming about the telescope. He was the dumbest, meanest, stingiest man I ever met and he's the only man I'd ever call nigger to his face, though I wouldn't actually do that because I'd rather die than say the word out loud, although I hear him say it all the time, knowing how much it makes white people uncomfortable.

But I told him he had no imagination or respect when he told me to keep my fingerprints off the watercolor ovals. "Just keep the fingers off the watercolor ovals" was all he could think up to say if I said anything.

But anyway, Dimitri was such a bad person, and Jimmy's notion of luxury seemed so innocent and ridiculous, that I was almost glad to see that chair there, even though I knew it had been bought off money made from pictures of Layla romping with trolls while Ambrosia rocked back and forth with her little cardboard book.

If you walk away from something that is complicated or hurts, no matter how simple your new place seems it's never long before it also starts getting complicated and full of things you couldn't have guessed at if somebody had asked up front. Things get complicated the way dropped things drop when you let them go. It's just how things are, how they go. I started understanding Rose's preference for religious vagaries—Lord, how long, how long, how long? She always meant how long before we get to heaven, I think. But if life goes on in heaven, I can't help but wonder how it doesn't get complicated there too. And once you're in heaven, there's no dying. So the question how long doesn't seem to make sense anymore. Sometimes it even feels to me a little bit like being stuck. But I know there's more to it than that. Or at least I feel there is. Or hope.

The Magazine Rack

You would be surprised at how much work it is to be poor. Nothing gives way to what you want. The winter is cold and you feel what that means. Summer is hot. Rain means your bed might get wet. Your clothes are thin and you know what it might be like not to have any clothes. There ain't nothing to steal, but people steal anyway because it's easy to steal from the poor. When we sat out on the porch and watched the train sometimes we were just getting over the work of being poor.

Church was the only beautiful thing in my life. And the baby that was growing inside me. And the jigsaw puzzle of Paris and the raccoon bones. And some other things I suppose. I haven't decided if a thing being beautiful is an idea or a feeling. I don't always feel very much that I know of. I've known people who cry and laugh and rage and they live their lives always doing one or the other of those things. But I know my baby got its stillness from me. I hardly feel anything at all sometimes. I do what's next. And that's the way the poor get their work done. That's the secret.

But every now and then, no matter how poor I was, I wanted to see something besides the house and Rose, Layla, Jimmy, and Ambrosia. I wanted to be alone, even though I was carrying around somebody. So I'd take a bath to make sure I smelled good. And then I'd go to the bookstore. Except for bus fare on the nights when Jimmy wouldn't drive me in his old nasty brown Chevy it didn't cost anything. I'd go to the bookstore to see the magazine rack.

It goes on and on and there are always people scattered along it looking at something. I can spend a whole Saturday night looking at magazines. It is a time I feel least and so I am the happiest. Almost everything I look at on the rack has to do with something besides me. I even sleep better knowing there is so much going on in the world besides me.

When I'm at the magazine rack I can't tell how many hours go by. There are so many things to look at and I have to breathe to keep myself looking at one at a time and not grabbing a bunch and seeming to cause trouble and getting thrown out. I have never once been thrown out.

Usually the other folks just leave me alone and that is when I am happiest. But sometimes I'll feel one of them stare when I reach for a magazine about hot rods or sculpture. It isn't mean, I can tell. And I know what I look like there. I am small except when my belly is big with the baby. My clothes are always clean but they're dingy. Why would I be reaching for a magazine about white men with mustaches who ride motorcycles? I understand their curiosity. But then they generally move on to their own magazines and leave me alone. I've learned how to stay calm and smile instead of getting nervous.

I'd rather people not look at me. So I don't look at them usually. But sometimes I do. I look at girls my age. I look at old people. Most everybody is white. When blacks are at the magazine rack they spend more time looking at me than white people do while I study Fly Fisherman or Coins or Cigar Aficionado. It's like they think they have a right.

"What are you staring at?" I want to say. But I don't. It would make everybody stare at us. Then we'd be a couple of black folks at the magazine rack. I'd as soon let it pass and let my mind drift off my shoulders and float colorless by the upper rack past the ideas of architecture or Italian fashions or war.

I don't feel a thing when I turn the pages of the magazines but I'm opening my eyes. I'm seeing what's what. Pretty soon I'll be telling this baby what's what and I better know. If it wasn't for the magazine rack what would I tell her? Here's the yard? Here's Jesus? Sorry the roof leaks? Watch out for the Troll under the Bare Sticks Bridge? That adds up to just about a big fat nothing.

And how long would that take anyway? No. There's got to be more. "You can talk about your heart," Rose said once when I started fretting about what I was gonna teach the baby. "You'll never get to the bottom of that," she said. But I must be almost half boy because I don't want to talk about my heart. I want to talk about why an arch doesn't fall in and who figured that out. I want to talk about how they check sugar levels in grapes when they make wine in France. I even want to talk about meat processing—I just don't want to see too many pictures of it.

I wish they gave a diploma for knowing everything at the magazine rack. I've learned more there than I ever learned in ninth grade. It's a wonder how many things people have thought up, like they can't help it. No matter how many times I go to the magazine rack, month after month, just when I worry over whether anything new can be thought up, there it is. And if I haven't gotten much done that month except just getting food cooked and the clothes clean, just getting done what needs to get done, I wonder how they find time to think all this up and to get it all into a magazine when they don't have any more hours in the day than I do. If there was one or two magazines, okay, but with hundreds busting open with new things that weren't there last month, it almost makes me think I wouldn't mind heaven and shouldn't worry over how long. Not that there is a magazine rack in heaven, which wouldn't make any sense. But something like it, something you never come to the end of and don't have to worry about coming to the end of since worrying over it would ruin it. That's all you need. That would be plenty.

Of course not all the magazines are about clean ideas or new ways to be happy or cook fish. Sometimes they're scary and I don't even know why, especially the ones with tattoos or very skinny women. I look at them anyway for some reason. Being raised in a crack house you just watch people put their nightmares on the outside. I've seen enough art magazines that, even though I wouldn't say anything about the crack house, if I could paint and had a big enough canvas, I might get a thing or two out about it.

Rich Man Walks By

Rose was dying but she still wanted to go outside on the porch and watch the train with her blanket over her knees. It was some work to get her out there but once she got on the sofa she looked around and felt the sunshine and she had the plain unsmiling look of being content. I know that feeling.

Off in the distance a ways we heard the train's whistle. So she'd get to watch the train right away before she got tired. She was so content she said, "I could do with a glass of lemonade," as though she forgot entirely that lemonade gave her heartburn with its acid. But I brought the lemonade and sat down.

We all five were sitting there waiting for the train for the first time in some months. I could see clear as day that Ambrosia was growing bigger and that made me see in a flash a picture of her being my size with everything that means and still rocking with her little cardboard book, probably with the colors nearly worn off from rubbing. What was Layla gonna do, I wondered, when Ambrosia got her period or when her body started feeling things that her brain wasn't ready for and never would be? But the train came and I didn't think long about it.

The train came and lasted about five minutes I guess. Rose didn't drink her lemonade. She just held it and let the coolness cool her hand. And she watched the train.

She was the first to say, "Now who's that?" when the train passed. There was a white man standing there on the tracks looking across at us. He had white hair and a fine gray suit. He had a tie and little gold bar running through his collar. His hands were in his pockets and he had one foot on a track and stared and stared like he was waiting for us to do something.

Rose said again, "Who do you suppose?"

He was like a ghost with all that white and gray, his clothes so fine, no scuffs on his black shoes, and he stared. It took me a few minutes to guess what he was there for but I think Jimmy and Layla knew right off. Layla stood up in her thin dress and walked over to the chicken-wire fence and leaned against one of the posts looking down the tracks like she wasn't paying the man any mind.

But you could tell he was paying her plenty of mind when he rubbed his strong chin with one of his hands.

When no one said anything Rose said, "He ain't the kind of man usually walks around here unless things changed while I been sick this winter. But I don't expect I been sick long enough for that much change. Is he lost you think?" And there was just the slightest bit of suspicion in that last question. Not much got past Rose when she was paying attention. I suppose she knew the heart well enough.

But the man after sort of hesitating walked on up the tracks, stepping with his expensive shoes only on the ties. Then he stepped off into the woods on the side where I knew there was a trail that led to a neighborhood.

"We need to fix up these houses," Jimmy said out of nowhere. "They's an eyesore anytime anyone comes walking by here."

Layla came back to the porch and sat down.

Rose said, "Jimmy? You know that man?" You could tell she was serious by the way she asked her question looking off into the distance instead of looking at Jimmy, like she was ready for anything and didn't want his grin to throw her off before she said what needed to be said.

He sat for a minute or so. "No, ma'am, I don't know him. But I wish I did." And we were all surprised by the way he said he wished he did. Who did he think he was talking to?

"Lord have mercy on you, Jimmy," Rose said. When she wanted to she had a way of summing up everything so that it made sense. But this seemed like more than she could make sense of. "You be careful. Yslea, you know that man? You know what Jimmy's talking about?"

"I don't know," I lied for the only time ever to Rose, not that I knew the man, so that wasn't a lie. But in my heart I was lying about the other question, the part about knowing what Jimmy was up to. That seemed like too much to talk about right then, and what could Rose have done about it anyway? Still, what Jimmy and Layla were doing to make money felt even worse now that it was not only happening but was being hidden on purpose from Rose. "You haven't touched your lemonade."

"I want to go inside, Yslea. I've had just about all the fresh air I can stand."

So I took her on inside, which took a while, and she didn't ask any more questions just then. I expect she was tired and knew that too many more questions would mean either a lot more work or a lot more worry. When you get old you have to pick and choose what you worry over for lack of time and energy, which you have to do anyway except that it's not so noticeable when you aren't old. You have to trust that some things that need to be worried over will be worried over by somebody with responsibility and in this case it was me.

When I came back out on the porch I asked Jimmy the same question whether he or Layla knew the man, in part to make up for the lie I told Rose but also because something needed to be done before things got out of hand. He gave the same answer. So I asked him how many people had signed up for that computer site. He said one hundred and seventy-six. And then he said, "I'm thinking I might quit the butcher shop." And that was when I knew they wouldn't stop. That was the warning sign of things to come. You don't just quit a skilled job like that. Not where I come from.

Stained Glass

I was working on my raccoon and Jimmy was gone and Layla and Ambrosia were inside doing whatever they did. Rose was laying on her narrow bed with her covers pulled up to her old breasts and then folded back neatly like she wanted to make sure that if she died there weren't any wrinkles in the sheet covering her. She had a thing about neatness and order and having no bugs around.

The day was so quiet and the sun dust was floating in the light that lit up Rose and the house was warming. I knew she was seeing the light through her closed eyelids and feeling the warmth. It was so quiet and calm that it made no sense to think of the rattlesnake under the house or the way some people seem to have a different set of rules than you for living.

So I worked on my raccoon and all sorts of ideas floated into my head and stayed there hovering just like the dust in the sunlight.

I hadn't cleaned the outside of the windows yet and so

they were stained with the dirt that blows up in storms and whatever small pieces of grime are carried from the air by raindrops so that everything smells fresh for a little while.

I almost had the spine worked out. The spine of a raccoon is a thing of wonder. Pure wonder. I took my time.

I took my time because I was starting to see that I was looking at a secret. Not just what bones look like when the flesh is gone but what it must be like to think up a raccoon. Looking at the bones makes you want to look at the muscle and the gristle and the nerves, not in a gross way but in a way that makes you see how it all fits together and works, with everything so neatly fit inside the fur like a suitcase you pack with everything you need for a week, nothing missing but no room left. And then on top of it all to put a face on it with details like whiskers, stripes, with eyes and a nose so that it looks around and finds its way in the world and has what it needs to get by, is like a good story in the form of an animal. One of my favorite parts about thinking about God making the world is that He put a face on everything that breathes, even though He didn't have to, which makes that part of the world so funny, except when it's scary, which actually is rare considering how many animals there are in the world compared to how many times I have been scared of one.

All of which is to say that jigsaw puzzle shapes make no sense. But the raccoon pieces made sense. Putting a face on everything that can handle one makes sense. And that's the idea that so got ahold of me.

Then there are other things that make sense, which you

already know about but don't pay attention to. Paying attention to a thing is different than just knowing it. It's the same as what they mean by something catching your eye except that it's the world catching your eye, not just a thing.

At night sometimes the quiet was damp like moldy dirt in a flower pot. And then when Jesus brayed it made me wonder at how hard it must be to be a beast and then I thought of Rose dying, then my still baby, and that I dreamed of things that I remembered in a foggy way.

But in the day's dusty sunlight the sun pushed away that fog and spread it like icing onto the ground and left the air clear.

In the church there is one stained-glass window high up above the altar. It's round and has all sorts of people, but except for Jesus I don't know who they are. But, even though I know they're famous and important, the colors around Jesus are just as important to me as the people. Even though the colors aren't part of His body they seem part of Him, like somebody's scent except that it's light instead of something you can smell. And in that window also the skin of Jesus, even though I'd bet it was meant to be white, isn't. It's more the color of my skin.

I thought of that and that was when I thought the light coming down on Rose might be even more wonderful passed through a stained-glass window and colored for the last ten feet of its journey from the sun. Which reminded me of how Rose was just full of wonder and excitement almost like a little kid when I told her one time when she was starting to look sad that I had read in a magazine on astronomy that light from the sun travels over ninety million miles to get to the Earth and that after all that distance you can just cover your eyes and block it from getting in. It's amazing that you can block something that has traveled so many miles, making shadows sort of interesting in a new way. But her response wasn't to make shadows to show how the sun's light can be pushed around. It was to lie perfectly still when the sun was in the window and to close her eyes and rest her arms beside her, which made her look dead, though she told me she was very happy with that piece of information I gave her. She told me I taught her something, even though you could've subtracted three of my lives from her life and still had some left over, and actually quite a lot I bet. I was not gonna ask her how old she was just in case it mattered, which I was sure it didn't to her. But the idea that I taught her something she didn't know even after all those years, I could have kissed her for telling me that, and did. She didn't open her eyes but just stayed calm and still in the sunlight, the way a cat does, or a plant.

When I thought about teaching a thought, I felt another thought akin to some of the others that had floated on in. I wondered how far the thoughts had traveled to reach me, though how far is not exactly what I mean. It's like when someone smiles at you, the smile has to travel from them to you, same as the sunlight, but the meaning of the smile, even though it gets to you from the other person doesn't travel across the room, but it still arrives. My thoughts felt like that, like something outside me that had arrived but not traveled.

But so did the baby growing up inside me without me doing anything to make it grow. Which I guess meant I ought to be careful when I talk about my baby or my thoughts because a fair amount of both seems to happen on its own and is not owned by anyone. I don't know.

I finished the spine just as these thoughts got confused. It was so orderly. I could hardly wait to hold my baby and run my fingers up and down her spine to feel the way it's put together while she slept on my chest.

The thing to do was not to think, not to try to make the thoughts come.

The light dropped with no effort at all. The thoughts would do the same.

The thing to do was to go about finding a stained-glass window. Which there were none that weren't being used. So next to the raccoon I cleared a space on the card table and I told Jimmy when he got home to pick up all the colored bottles he could find, whole or broken. He moaned but nodded, which he knew was the least he could do after all the ways he'd changed everything without asking anybody first.

I would glue pieces of glass to a piece of clear plastic and hang it over the window. I knew exactly what I would do and it was even better than taking care of Rose after she was dead, which of course I would still do anyway. I would make her a beautiful place to die.

Medicine Bottles

I knew that when the baby came I would not have so much time to think and for sure I'd be thinking different thoughts then. So what I thought about was that this was the last time I could think the thoughts of a person who doesn't have a child. But so much was different with her inside me that I had already started thinking like a mother, which means I missed the moment I changed. It doesn't bother me because we miss a lot of moments that are important to us, when we're babies or even being born, and they happen anyway. Which is a good thing because if we had to pay attention to every moment that matters to us for it to happen none of us would be here. That's a thought I like since it takes the pressure off me to notice everything, though my brain will keep noticing and chattering on and on about things.

There was only so much time I could fiddle with raccoon bones and think my thoughts so once while she was asleep I went and looked at Rose's pills. Rose had all sorts of pills on her nightstand. I'd never seen her take a single pill and so I started thinking maybe it made her feel better having them there just in case. They were all from years ago and the bottles were all half empty.

I figured the old bottles of medicine were sort of like the bug spray that made the house smell so chemical. They were some kind of protection, some kind of thing they'd made to make life better, and she felt good having some of it even if it was old.

The newest bottle was from ten years ago and I figured she hadn't been to a doctor since then. Likely she kept the medicine for a time when she'd really need it. Whatever kind it was. Likely to Rose medicine was medicine. Bug spray kills all bugs. Medicine kills all the germs in your body that make you sick.

There was something about all her medicine bottles and bug spray that made me sad. It reminded me of when my mama was dying.

I never tried crack and I never will. And as far as I can tell that's the only difference between me and my mama. I don't hate her. But when I was a kid more than one person told me to leave and more than one person has told me they can't believe I came up in the house I came up in because of the nice way I act.

But once Mama was dying she had a whole bunch of pill bottles around her. Which was strange to me then and is now because she got her disease because of what she had to do to get her crack and then took her crack to get away from that memory and then took medicine to stay alive in the middle of it all. To stay alive long enough to have more crack I guess. She was not dumb. But she would only go to the doctor to get her pills. Once she had her pills she had no use for the doctor. "Go to the doctor for what?" she'd say. "To let them look at you," somebody'd say, maybe a visiting minister, maybe a Democrat. But she'd just turn her head toward the wall.

I used to sit by her bed and roll her pill bottles down a ramp then push them up again using two fingers like legs and let them roll down again while I waited for her to wake up. Sometimes she'd look at me like she was wondering why I was there staring at her. But sometimes she'd smile and that's why I'd sit there for hours rolling those pill bottles to be doing something even if it was boring. It was worth it.

She came close to death or what looked like death to me a hundred times using crack. But then one day death obliged her and came close without her asking. And I could see in her eyes a new kind of fear that scared me.

That was why I didn't mind staying with Rose while she died. There was no fear in her eyes. There was nothing scary about her pills. She was dying of what you're supposed to die of. And the room where she was gonna die was so pleasant and quiet. There was plenty of room for me to mull over things and to be sad and to do my work.

"Yslea. Yslea, can you get me a glass of cold water?"

"Yes, ma'am," I said.

My baby sort of moved a little then and then went back to sleep. If I didn't know the difference I'd say it felt like no more than my stomach grumbling when she moved. But it meant so much to me even if it only felt like that. Just knowing she was there.

What Jimmy Found in the Garbage Can

When I first saw Jimmy on the porch I thought he was tough, the way he sat with his feet wide apart and his hands dangling across his thighs and the way he stared at the treetops that made him look like he was mad about something. And then I got to thinking he was boring, moving back and forth between the computer and the butcher shop. Then when this baby started growing I thought maybe Jimmy was just what it is to be grown and work. Then I decided he was greedy and small while he worked Layla's gift.

But sometimes he made me wonder. Like when he brought pork chops home. Or when he agreed to collect colored glass so I could make a window fit for Rose's last days of looking at the sun. And it wasn't just that he picked up the bottles and broken glass but that he washed them off and smoothed the edges before he put them in a shoe box for me.

It only took him a couple of weeks to get me probably

fifty pieces of glass, all different shapes and colors. I was still thinking about how to attach them to the piece of clear plastic I found. Jimmy said glue them but I didn't know what kind of glue and he said he'd find out. And that's what I'm talking about. Somehow he wasn't bad through and through, even though if you saw his web site you'd have to think he was evil.

At first the colors were what you'd probably expect. Pieces from brown and green beer bottles because those are everywhere. You just have to look down to find them. He would take bottle bottoms and flat pieces of glass and knock the sharp parts off, then rub the edges against a brick to smooth them a bit and then put them in soapy water to soak. Then he found a couple of blue ones from bath oil or some such thing and I started to think about what you might say about the bottles. Some were from drunks lying around wasting their lives or else just doing everything they could so they didn't notice their lives. And some were probably from lovers trying to get over being scared of the size of what they were feeling. But most I had no idea about. Especially when he started finding some fancy glass that had to come from the kind of bottles you see in the same magazines as those skinny women in silly clothes that I think would make me nervous if I ever saw a person like that in real life. He got me the round and sometimes square bottoms of purple, yellow, silver, gray, black, orange, white, lime, you name it.

I got to where I enjoyed just pulling out the shoe box full of colored glass and looking into it and feeling the smooth weight of each piece. A kind of treasure. But I still meant to make the window.

I couldn't tell you where all he found the glass but I know he kept his eyes open all the time looking and even though it didn't just fix everything he'd done it was somehow nice thinking about him thinking about what I wanted while he walked along.

Then one day he was on Rose's porch knocking the sharp edges off a red piece of glass the color of a pomegranate seed and he seemed jumpy and upset, which Jimmy never was. They don't make many red bottles so I thought this piece ought to go in the center like an eye and I wanted to glue it on right away to get the window started. But Jimmy said he wanted to wash it some more. And after he had washed it again and again with soap he said he hoped I had enough for my window. I said I did, but why. And he said that he wasn't looking for glass in garbage cans anymore.

He had to reach past something dead to get the red bottle. He did it before he even thought about it and then he felt sick. Maybe it was a dead cat. "It's only a thought," I told him. But he shook his head. I could tell he thought maybe it was something worse. And he had reached right past it hardly thinking at first.

I pointed out that he spent all day up to his elbows in dead things and didn't seem to mind it. He said this was different and then wouldn't talk about it anymore.

So I thanked him and didn't ask and I took my red glass to the box and began to plan. Now I had my two boxes. One with raccoon parts and one with the pieces of glass each from a different kind of story.

And I had new things to think about. The difference between one dead thing and another dead thing for example. And the fact that the difference matters.

I laid down my square piece of plastic next to the board where I had put together the raccoon's spine.

I started to place the pieces of glass here and there quietly so as not to wake Rose.

There was a rule to guide putting together the raccoon and it was a rule I hadn't made up, which I liked. But I was not sure yet about the stained-glass window. There might be a rule because I knew without a doubt that the thick red round piece belonged in the middle and that didn't feel like something I made up but instead how it ought to be. And if that was so, why wouldn't there be a way to know where the other pieces ought to be?

WHITE MAN WITH TATTOOS

Over time even if you don't want to be part of a thing you can start to notice patterns. I tried not to pay much attention to Layla and Jimmy but after a while there was this one white man I thought might just move in with her. I didn't trust him. Not because he was white. Because he wasn't natural.

For one thing he was covered in tattoos. At least the parts I had seen, which included his chest and back since he often didn't wear a shirt. I was curious as the next person about what tattoos might be in the more private areas but I wouldn't ever peek. And when I thought about it, it made me a little sick.

For another thing his eyes. His eyelids were sort of slits and his eyes were blue but they were dull and didn't focus. It was like when he looked at you it was with a secret eye fixed on the bridge of his nose so his head was always tipped back just a little bit.

His skin wasn't white like most white skin, which a lot of times has a good bit of brown or red or pink in it to make it look real. His skin was the white of wax paper. And his veins ran underneath the tattoos like sewer lines and made the waxy skin look like marble. His chest was all thin and caved in so with his tipped head he looked like he was rearing back ready to strike. Which was distracting if he was saying "Yes, ma'am," and "No, ma'am," like he did to me, though I was sure I was a good bit younger than he was. I don't trust it when a man does that. A woman I can understand. Not a man.

He came by two weeks in a row on Tuesdays. Then he came a couple of days in the same week and I hadn't ever asked Layla if she had a rule but like I said, you watch long enough and you see patterns and this wasn't part of the pattern. He was taking more days than fit the way Layla usually did things, like kids grabbing more than one tangerine before they see if there's enough to go around. He had a scraggly beard but he kept it short and he didn't carry his bags with him so I figured he must not be one of the ones who are wanderers like most.

Then he did something I'd never seen any of them do. He came by while Layla was with somebody and Jimmy told him Layla was resting but he sat down on the porch leaning against the porch post, not on Jimmy's porch or Layla's but mine and Rose's.

What do you do when a scraggly-looking white man sits on your porch and then, like he just thought of it, asks if it's okay if he sits? Everybody knows that's worse than just sitting down because it makes you answer with yes or no and neither makes you feel good. So I just didn't answer and looked off in a different direction.

I wished Jimmy would jump in and say that's not the way we do things but he just sat in his easy chair and stared across the tracks feeling the breeze like nothing was happening. Still, I could tell from his face that he was thinking and wondering what to do.

The marble man talked and talked about nothing at all so you couldn't even think your own thoughts. And he'd say something that wasn't even funny and then he'd laugh and look at us and since it wasn't funny I didn't laugh so he shook his head like I was stupid and didn't understand the funny thing he had said.

If he'd done that a few more times I just might have said something but then the train came and for a minute he kept moving his mouth but when he saw that no one could hear him, even though it's a lot quieter once the engine passes, he shut up and let the train pass. And he shook his head again like the train had done something stupid by passing by.

About the time the train had passed one of Layla's bums came out and didn't even look at us but he looked at the marble guy like he was scared and then walked on through the gate and down the track looking back over his shoulder every now and then, carrying his nasty bags with him. He was so filthy I couldn't even tell what color he was.

"Can I bother you for a glass of water, ma'am?" the tattoo man asked me. I didn't say anything but I got up, maybe making a little too much fuss in my struggle to stand up to show it's not so easy when you're pregnant, and I got him his glass of water.

"Much obliged," he said with a grin I didn't like and he drank it down in four swallows with his head tipped back and his pointy Adam's apple bobbing up and down.

Just then Layla and Ambrosia came out on the porch and I saw in a flash that Layla wished she hadn't come out. She looked a little bit tousled and she said, "Not today."

The marble guy said, "How do, Layla," and then he stood up and walked over to Ambrosia. "And how's the little lady?" And he started tickling her while she was looking at her book and she didn't look at him but she jerked away and when he tried again she jerked away again and screamed.

"Leave her be," Layla said.

Then he kind of laughed and said, "All right, some other time." And he walked away still chuckling to himself. He walked, head tipped back, laughing at the sun.

For a long time nobody said anything. Then I said, "I'd just as soon he didn't come around here anymore," because somebody had to say something.

"It's a free country," Jimmy said.

"Is it?" I asked him. That made me so mad I could've popped.

The marble man's glass was sitting there on the porch. I decided right there I'd throw it away instead of washing it. I didn't even want to pick it up.

Bruised Sky

Some things and people can become part of your dreams just by being made up the way they are. The rattlesnake can easy enough. The sound of the train passing by at night. The Troll under the bridge. The rich man standing with his white shirt and cuff links in the middle of the track. But somehow none of these seem evil. Snakes can't help what they are. The Troll—well, nobody with any real power good or bad stays under a bridge. Stay away from the bridge and you stay away from the Troll. And the rich white man was from another world than mine.

But the tattooed marble man with the wax-paper skin grabbed on to the hem of one of my dreams and he wouldn't let go. He didn't do much. He didn't need to. He just needed to grin and turn his dull eyes up here and there and drink his water, leave his glass, walk around with his shirt off, all white and waxy and covered in nasty tattoos.

Between that and not getting into a comfortable position all night with the baby I hardly could sleep and finally I got up and waited for the sun to come up. It was the first time since I was a girl and got locked out of the house that I saw the sunrise.

Sitting in the dark when it's almost time for the sun is so different from sitting in the dark when the only thing you have to look forward to is more dark.

So I watched the sky to see if it had changed since I was a girl.

My father was one of who knows how many men who were in and out of the house. I don't know which one. But I would guess he was white. I say that because my mother had dark skin and it would take a lot of white to get skin to my shade in one step.

It wasn't until I was about thirteen and my mama died that I really noticed how different our color was and the shapes of our noses. I was kneeling by her bed listening to her groan. I almost never got to really look at her except when she was sick and even then I wouldn't have stared except that it was my mama. There was not much peace between us for most of the time I can remember and when she was sick it looked like peace from the outside but mostly it was just being sick, which makes it hard to do anything good or bad except for moaning.

I didn't hate her but I didn't really need her either. I had stopped needing her long before that. If I needed her I'd have hated her. But speaking as a grown-up with a baby, it's the saddest thing I can think of not to need your mama. And it was sad to see how weak she was, even though when she got mad she seemed so strong and huge to a little girl.

I guess the hardest thing about living in a crack house was just getting people to leave you alone. But that's one thing I'll say for Mama. Lord, even if she wasn't so high she couldn't see straight and one of those men started messing with me she wouldn't ask any questions before she was screaming and hitting and throwing things and looking for her baseball bat and pretty soon I was safer than most because it wasn't worth the trouble messing with me. I was always happy when she protected me like that, though truth be told I'm pretty sure those men were on the receiving end of her bat because of anger that was older than me. Still, I felt a lot better than I might have if she hadn't stood up for me.

There was one girl we knew named Manganese who was four years old when she got AIDS and she died when she was seven. I don't think Mama had it then but after Manganese got it people including Mama were pretty upset about the thought of getting it and not being able to do much about it. The way a smoker probably feels about lung cancer.

But the night I was locked out and nobody was straight or sober enough to hear me knocking and find the door and let me in I sat up against the front of the house with my legs crossed and didn't go to sleep all night. And when the sun started to come up I had become someone new and a lot of the change in me I don't think I had much to do with, like being born. It was then that I stopped even thinking about needing anybody. I looked at the sky and saw it was purple and red and it looked like a great big bruise. And then the whole bruised injured sky burnt away and became orange and then a calm blue. And those were the colors of my youth.

And once I escaped the tattooed wax-paper man in my nightmare I saw the same colors in the sky. The same colors in the sky like seeing the moon and knowing someone a hundred miles away can see the same moon. Except that it wasn't two people looking at the same colors at the same time. It was me looking at the same colors at two different times. My life had settled somewhere else but it was slowly feeling all of a piece.

But even after that night I changed I still had whole drawers full of hurt. And they could be opened when I didn't know to expect it. In eighth grade science class when I learned that manganese was an element. In ninth grade history class when I learned about a place called Krakow, which sounded to me like crack house.

People did not understand why I would start to cry. I did not want to make them understand.

The whole time I sat out on the porch after I couldn't sleep, Jesus stood in the yard. I didn't know whether or not he was asleep but I felt safe and good.

Circus Show

It seems to me that sometimes the world feels empty like it's lit up by fluorescent lights instead of by the sun. And other times so much seems stuffed into it that the change of one thing, anything, can't help but change something about another thing, anything, everything. Like the raccoon where everything stuffed inside his fur is needed, with nothing extra and no room for anything else. Everything working together.

But the morning I watched the bruised sky heal, I just kept sitting. I knew everyone would be awake soon because the train would come by. I waited for it.

Three engines pulled it so I knew it would be a long one. It started slowing down before it got to me. I watched as the gray cars started slowing down, carrying whatever it is they carry. I saw the man in the window of the first engine but he didn't wave and neither did I, more like we were looking at a painting of each other instead of each other, which was fine since it was so early in the morning when everything is still hazy either from sleep or no sleep.

When it finally came to a stop I had one of those feelings. By this time the cars in front of me were painted red and yellow. They were from a circus. Some of them held rides, one after another on down the track. But the one right in front of me held some of the animals. At first I couldn't see what all kinds of animals it held but I heard an elephant.

Every dog in hearing range did too. They set to barking and howling. Jesus stood by the fence with his neck against the chicken wire, staring.

The way the car was made it had slits along the sides for air. I could see animal bodies or at least strips of hide up against the slats and they cried out.

I wondered where the elephant was from.

When I think of the circus I think about how it's a place where nothing is normal. The animals act different than anywhere else. And the people do too. It's a place where freaks can finally be normal. I've never seen a circus except on television but that's enough for me to understand some things about circuses and what the people and the animals have to be like to be in a circus every day.

I remember when I was a kid. For a while I was bused to a school with mostly white kids. But it wasn't my skin that made me feel different since it's so light. It was my one dress and two pairs of pants that were exactly the same color so that people thought I was wearing the same pair all the time and for some reason said so to my face. When I moved over to the black school I didn't feel like I stood out for being light-skinned, which made me see how black I must have felt in the white school, even though I didn't know it. But also my clothes didn't make me stand out either.

I wished Ambrosia would come out and look at the animals but I can't say she would notice them even if she was standing right beside one.

In some ways Ambrosia makes me sadder than even myself when I think about myself as a kid. There were lots of times when from the outside I looked a lot like Ambrosia just to keep everyone away. I didn't have a book of colors but I did have a Great Book of World Transportation with all sorts of cars, trains, airplanes, and ideas about the future of hovercraft and electric cars and space travel. I loved that book and all I wanted was to be left alone.

But Ambrosia is different because she can't seem to come out of her book.

She's like a circus, always looked at from the outside. She is a whole world all by herself. Her whole world fits in the book of colors like the five train cars lined up with the whole world of the circus in them.

When the engines that were so far past they were on around the curve in the tracks began to pull forward the cars all jerked against each other like a wreck and all the animals screamed at once.

For an animal I can't think of anyplace more different from its home than a train car. And what home for Ambrosia would look like if she wasn't the way she is I do not know.

But as long as the wax-paper man stayed away I started thinking home for me looked just like what I was living. Like life with Rose, then life in Rose's house raising a person and figuring out things that I could work on and think about and do.

Drop of Blood in a Glass of Milk

I started my day's work feeding bread with butter and sugar on it to Rose. Even when she was feeling bad she'd eat bread with butter and sugar on it.

But she must have had a fitful night too because she ate one piece and wanted to go back to bed.

So I took the other piece with me into the kitchen and poured a glass of milk. I was sitting there with my head hanging down over the glass of milk looking at how white it was. Nothing else was going through my mind except how white the milk was, even though normally I'd be thinking about how they organize everything you need to get a glass of milk, everything from cows to glue machines that close up the carton, though that last part needs some work since half the time you can't get the spout open after the first step of opening the carton. But all I was thinking about was white.

Then a drop of blood fell from my nose into the glass of milk. As soon as it hit the milk, pink ran out to the edges and I didn't care at the moment how it was pretty because it scared me. Women know a lot more about blood than men and if you want someone to help you with a bloody nose you got in a fight or a toenail that got pulled back when you stubbed your toe, go to a woman. But those things are expected. I hadn't picked my nose or anything, so this was different. Blood in an unexpected place is scary. Especially if it shows up when you are paying attention to the white of milk and for once not thinking about anything else.

No more blood dropped. I held a napkin to my nose just in case. But mostly I stared at the pink milk.

I began to feel afraid like this was a sign that something bad was gonna happen. Or worse, that something bad had already happened that couldn't be changed. The same as there is no way to get the pink out of the milk.

It wasn't like being afraid of the man with tattoos or any one thing. Like dying. Or the baby dying, though you might think my first thought was that it was a sign about the baby since that would make sense.

It was just fear.

I ate the bread with butter and sugar on it and waited to see what would happen next.

And what happened was that I asked myself what I have that matters, which was not what I expected to happen. But fear does that sometimes. At the white school the principal used to come to class and read us Robinson Crusoe. I felt like everybody looked at me when he started talking about Friday and I tried to think how I could ask for a bathroom pass without everybody staring at me more. But pretty soon

I just wanted to hear the story. After that it was my favorite time of the school day and before he came I always made sure my notebooks were in my desk and my pencils were in the sandwich bag I had to carry my stuff in and everything was neat because I just wanted to listen. After a few weeks when the story was finished all I wanted was for the principal to start over, even though I knew he was gonna move to the next class since our teacher had told us this was his way to let us get to know him and we should behave when he came. So when he read the last line and closed the book and everybody clapped and started putting together their stuff to go home, I did the same because it's important not to just sit there since people will ask you why you are just sitting there and I didn't want to say I was thinking about the story. But when I got my stuff together and started to walk out, I didn't know why but the principal came over to me and gave me his copy of the book, and he didn't say anything to me but that I know how to listen to a story and he would be honored if I would have his copy, and I was as happy as I have ever been. I wished I could tell him that that was the reason I didn't say thank you or say anything else but just stood there holding the book, then put it in my paper sack and smiled and ran, because he probably couldn't figure out that it was the first book anybody gave me that I did not have to give back, including the Great Book of World Transportation, which I found in the house but which technically did not belong to me.

That night I opened it up as carefully as if it had money

in it and I started reading it. I especially liked the beginning because when he found himself on an island by himself he didn't do what I would have done back then, which is to get all worried about this and that, but instead he made a list of what he had.

So I looked at my glass of pink milk and thought about what I had. And first I thought fear. I had fear. And I could look at it and wonder about it and feel it. Which added wonder and feeling to the list.

Most everything else I had was inside the house. I had the raccoon and all my thoughts about how it's to be put together. I had my stained-glass window that I was thinking about, which was beautiful in my mind. I had Rose, who was dying and who would give me this house. I had the baby from Jimmy. Then there was Jesus walking around in the yard, the only living thing that could nuzzle Ambrosia without being hit. There was Jimmy. And there was Layla's dark heart.

So my list was this: a kind of fear, a kind of wonder, a kind of feeling, a kind of order, a kind of beauty, death, birth, my story, sin. And God. I needed to go up and get the bread and the wine. I needed the body and the blood. I needed the resurrection of the Lord. That's jumping right into it. Not running away but letting it sweep right over you. The body and the blood.

I took up my glass of pink milk and I drank it down. All the way. And I wiped my mouth on my arm. It seemed like there was nothing I could do about the fear, but plunging right into it made me feel better. I had so much to think about that a life didn't seem long enough to get through it all. I started to wish I'd finished high school so I could go to college and learn about this. But how could that ever happen? I would have to sort things on my own. The way Rose did.

SWIRL

Once Jimmy got our houses painted they looked a lot better. It didn't help the way everything leaned but the white paint made the places look fresh and clean.

We were sitting out on our porches and the breeze was blowing. Rose was getting weaker I could tell. She didn't say anything about the paint. I don't know if she couldn't see it or smell it but I figured she knew where Jimmy got the money.

Jimmy started talking about other things he could do to improve business. He was talking in front of Rose like he didn't care if she heard. Maybe he thought she didn't even know what a computer was. Maybe he was getting a little too big for his britches.

He started talking about the fence, about how it needed to be something besides chicken wire. And he thought Jesus ought to spend more time in the field and less time around the yard. Every time he was putting new pictures and movies on the web site and Jesus was stretching to stick the tip of his nose through the window to sniff he just felt unprofessional, he said.

I noticed that more well-dressed men seemed to be wandering down the tracks every now and then. I guess Layla was becoming a kind of adventure to a certain kind of restless man.

I told Jimmy it bothered me, all those strangers just walking into the yard.

"That's nothing new," he said.

But I said I meant the ones in suits. I wasn't so worried about the bums. They seemed to be Layla's life work. But I said right in front of Layla, shouldn't there be some morals about the thing?

Layla had on another new dress at the time and she knew I was looking at her. She just looked away, which I felt bad about since to tell the truth she wasn't the one who came up with all this and never asked anybody for anything that I heard of except to be left alone when she was out on her couch, and she didn't even ask for that but just made it so anybody could guess that was what she wanted by sitting as far away as she could get unless the sun was in her eyes. She almost never talked anymore, even less than she used to.

And what about the man the color of wax paper with tattoos? I asked Jimmy.

He said that he heard he had been stabbed to death near

Blues Alley. Which didn't help me any because Jimmy was always hearing about this or that and since only half of it turned out to be true it was like he didn't say anything at all worth listening to because you could say any of those things yourself and then just flip a coin and get the same fifty-fifty chance of being right.

Anyway, the man hadn't showed up since the day he sat on the porch, thank God. If he was dead it made me even gladder that I threw away the glass he used. But he's not entirely gone, I guarantee it. I can't prove it but I am sure he's the one who made Layla sick.

All of sudden while we were talking the winds came just right and formed a little swirl of dust in the yard and picked up the dry leaves from the corners. And then while they swirled, for the first time I've ever seen, Ambrosia jumped up and ran into the swirling leaves and began to turn in a circle with her arms out.

And just as quick as it started the wind moved on and Ambrosia stood for a long time in the yard with her arms limp by her sides and head hanging down.

It was that swirling motion that caught my mind. I thought of a dog chasing its tail. And the shape of the swirl on a snail's shell. And the way the toilet flushes.

She came on back to the porch and sat down with her legs all tangled up underneath her and she started to rock, first with her little usual rocking motion that I had gotten used to and then with bigger rocking motions, then bigger.

Then we all saw at the same time that she wasn't holding her book of colors.

She rocked and nothing was happening yet. But Ambrosia without her book of colors isn't right. It doesn't work. We all knew it, and sure enough we were right.

The Troll Visits Just in Time

Once she started screaming it was hard to talk about who was going up under the porch to get her book. I said I was pregnant and couldn't fit. Jimmy said he'd already gone after the rattlesnake once and there was no way he was gonna be up under the porch with it. He said Layla was her mama and she ought to get up under there. But Layla, who had listened to Ambrosia scream more than any of us, was used to it so she just sat and thought for a while. Since she had on one of her new dresses I knew she didn't want to get it dirty.

But that little cardboard book was about all that girl had. She's the kind who's just as well off poor as rich since everything except the book is wasted on her.

Just when I was about to go inside to get away from her screaming if Layla wasn't gonna do anything about it I looked up and saw the Troll standing by the fence with his wild hair and beard full of twigs. He looked like he was half man half tumbleweed. And he stared right at Layla and had these little jerks of his shoulders which I guessed were chuckles.

Now that he was out from under his bridge he didn't look so big. In fact, in the light I figured even I could take him, he was so scrawny-looking. This was the first time I'd seen him walking around in the real world. I had stopped walking all the way to the bridge since I'd seen him that first time.

He kept staring at Layla. I could see his lips moving but I couldn't hear because of Ambrosia. I figured he was saying, "Give us some of that, give us some of that," and then snickering.

As Layla was getting rich she was also getting full of herself to my eye. She sat there like she was deciding all sorts of things for other people—Ambrosia, us, even the poor old Troll half embarrassed I'd say at us staring at him, knowing all about what he wanted.

Then Layla motioned for the Troll to come over to her like she was a queen or worked at a bank, which wouldn't have been bad if it was one of those newer types of men coming by but this was a poor old thing who everybody could tell was nervous even just being out from under his bridge.

He came over all trembling. I couldn't hear what Layla said to him but when she finished he danced a little jig in the yard, then crawled up under the porch and came out with Ambrosia's book. What I liked was that he didn't hand it to her so that she'd have to reach toward him and take it, which most people would do but she didn't like to for some reason. Instead he laid it down beside her and even seemed to make a little bow when he stepped away, which made the grunts he kept making seem more like just something he couldn't help instead of something he was doing on purpose.

I figured what Layla'd offered him. He must have heard of her from some bum passing over his bridge or crawling up under it during a rain, and if I was right about him mostly just staying up under the bridge I imagine it took some courage for him to make his way down to Layla's house and stare until she called him over.

I wasn't scared of him just then so I said out of curiosity and trying to be friendly, "Did you see our rattlesnake up under the house?"

He chuckled. Then his face was serious. Then he chuckled again. Then he seemed confused.

Layla stood and opened her door and said for him to come on inside. She stood waiting.

He looked like he was counting on his fingertips and he counted and counted and counted.

"Well?" Layla said in her new haughty way. I didn't like it.

We all waited with her to see what the nasty Troll would do, although like most people once you see more of them he was not just the nasty Troll to my mind anymore because not only had he gotten the book but he had paid attention to something not just everybody would pay attention to about Ambrosia. He put his hands in his pockets and stood a while longer. I guess he was waiting to see what he would do too.

And Layla said, "You comin' or not?" like she had all sorts of things to do that day instead of just sitting in her new dress at the end of the couch like the rest of us. Maybe it was because I wasn't sleeping because of the baby that I sometimes felt a little irritable but I almost said something.

Then some kind of decision was made inside him and instead of going inside he ran back to the chicken-wire fence and jumped over. He looked around sort of crouching like he was expecting somebody to follow him. Then he ran off, probably to Bare Sticks Bridge where he lived his strange little life.

"He's not a paying customer," Jimmy said right away like he'd been thinking it all along before anybody else said anything.

"He got Ambrosia's book back," Layla answered. Then she said, "You don't own me, Jimmy. Don't you never forget that."

She almost looked disappointed that the Troll didn't come in. The only thing I can think of worse than being with the Troll is being with the wax-paper man. But Layla seemed somehow hungry for the filthiest man she could find. So calm. And she was always clean. She hardly ever sweated. Maybe it was because her womb was taken out that she didn't sweat.

But all this made me think about how the Troll showed up exactly when Ambrosia danced in the wind and dropped her book of colors under the porch. That's exactly the kind of thing my brain talks to me about all the time.

Theories of Time

That night I had to go look at magazines at the bookstore to get my mind clear of things. I went thinking I might even buy a magazine about raising babies. All the ones I saw had white women raising their white babies. Which I don't mind so much except that the baby was so much a part of my body that I'd just as soon have a magazine that says something about what to do when she notices that almost everything that seems to matter around her is white and she isn't.

I don't know why but also almost everybody is white in the hot-rod magazines, the porno magazines, the economics magazines, and the foreign magazines.

That's why I sometimes look through the science magazines. There are almost never pictures of people. Just fish and molecules and math.

So that night when I didn't find the baby magazine I wanted—and I didn't have money anyway, I could have asked Jimmy but didn't like that idea—I found a science magazine and on the cover was a title "Theories of Time" in big block letters. The picture on the front had a clock, some stars, a picture of two airplanes flying toward each other, and the slice of a tree with its rings.

I started reading the magazine article, which turned out to be about something different than what I decided I would mean when I made my own Theory of Time.

It was the way things sometimes seem to just come together that I wanted to know about and put into my theory. I wanted my theory to be about what brought the Troll to our yard at the right time. About the difference between what I feel in summer and what I feel in winter and what the clock says all the time. About how much time "all the time" is. About that Rose's time was coming, which meant she'd be dead, Jimmy's time was coming, which meant he'd be rich, and my time was coming, which meant I'd be a mama.

So I got what I wanted at the magazine stand—something to think about—even if I didn't get a magazine. And it was one of those things that no matter how much you think about it even at the beginning of thinking, you have a hunch that you will never get to the end of the thought and instead of that being discouraging it's actually exciting because it's the thinking about it that feels good instead of just the coming to the end of the idea.

While I was waiting outside for Jimmy to come pick me up I thought about the time my baby was spending inside me. I thought about the kind of time you see in dreams. I wondered what Ambrosia's time must be like. It was about to change, that much I knew. That would be something I'd need to watch. To tell the truth my body had started turning into a woman's body when I was ten years old and I can tell you that, even though I knew some things, I wasn't ready for that. They talk about a woman's clock ticking. But it's true even for girls. Even if Ambrosia never thought about time, her body sure would keep track of time, and then what was gonna happen to her?

By the time Jimmy came I had already figured out something I hadn't known that morning. That there are all sorts of time to think about. And that's why I love the rows and rows of magazines. Whole worlds, each one of them. And sometimes everything just comes together. Like the book of colors dropping, the Troll, Theories of Time.

All this went to the back of my brain I have to say when Jimmy drove up in a yellow Cadillac with a white roof and nodded for me to get in. The dashboard and speedometer and lights looked like the airplane cockpits I'd seen in flying magazines and the steering wheel was polished wood instead of plastic. At first I couldn't say anything. I felt like I was sitting in a nice restaurant with three forks like the one I used to wash dishes in. I wasn't comfortable. But Jimmy, he hadn't had the car two hours and he was already driving with one hand and with his seat tipped back and a hat on.

"Where'd you get this car? Where's the old car?"

"I left it on the side of the road. It's junk. I ain't driving junk, not anymore."

"Where'd you get this car?"

Then he said, "Baby, my time has come."

When he said one of the things about time that I had just been thinking—well, that needed a whole other day to think it through.

Can't Have More Than One

The book was nothing. A few cardboard pages folded, stapled with two staples. Each page was a different color—green, black, red, white, gold.

Before Layla got so uppity she told me where it came from. They were at church and Layla was just figuring out there was something bad wrong with her girl. She never went to a doctor, just got her shots at the health department. But the ladies there said she ought to get the girl to a doctor. That something wasn't right.

Of course Layla had this much figured out on her own. But just about the time she thought maybe she'd go the emergency room and ask a doctor what was wrong with Ambrosia, why she was so cold and didn't pay attention and screamed a lot, a nursery worker at the church found out something.

It was an old lady in the nursery who smiled at Layla when she dropped off Ambrosia like she knew she was giving

Layla a break and that was what she did on Sunday morning instead of going to the service, which was a wonderful thing to my mind. Ambrosia would sit in the corner and face the wall and rock and scream. They'd put one toy after another in front of her but she wasn't interested. She'd just rock and scream the whole time Layla was in church.

Then one day Layla came to the nursery after church to pick up Ambrosia and she didn't hear any screaming. She surprised me a little bit when she told me she felt good because she thought maybe Ambrosia had run away. She was so tired. Then she felt bad about feeling that. What surprised me wasn't that she felt it. Anyone could understand that. It was that she told me at all, just in passing.

But Ambrosia hadn't run away. She was just quiet for the first time. And there she was, over in the corner while the rest of kids played together, facing the wall, rocking, turning the pages of that little cardboard book of colors. The old lady grinned and shrugged her shoulders. She'd had this little book in her purse, she said, and didn't know what to do when just then Jesus told her to give it to Ambrosia. And look.

Layla didn't even have to ask before the old lady said, "Now you just take that book on with you." I guess that was three years ago when Ambrosia was three.

I think the book is a little world with just a few colors and one shape. But whole, like an alphabet with only five letters. Maybe it's all the world she can stand. It means something.

But one day I was at church and I saw the old lady who took care of the nursery. So I went over to her and I felt like I was about to talk to somebody who I'd heard about on the radio because I knew how important what she had done for Layla was. I asked her if she remembered giving Ambrosia that book of colors.

"Lord, yes," she said. She must have been about Rose's age, but happier.

"Where'd you get it?" I asked her.

"Sunday school," she answered. Then she took me over to the closet where the Sunday-school supplies were kept and opened it up. She pulled out a shoebox and took off the top. "See. We got a lot of them."

The box was full of those little cardboard books of color.

"See, the colors mean different things. Growth. Sin. The holy blood of our Lord and Savior Jesus Christ, blessed be His name. And glory to God, the mansions made of pearl and gold where we all shall find our rest." She eyed me for a minute to see if I was caught up in the message like she was. Then she looked down at my pregnant stomach and she broke into a big smile like old ladies do when they are remembering things and she asked me, "You want one? Here, take a couple."

I almost did but I just couldn't do it. That book was too important to Ambrosia for there to be another one around. I don't understand it all but it just seemed like if there was another one around, or two, or fifty, it would be too much. It would ruin it somehow.

On the way home that day I wondered why sin had to be black. I wish I knew more about the meaning of color. I wish I knew more about everything.

Air Conditioning

With maybe a month to go, and being so big in my belly and so small everywhere else, I felt the heat of spring in the South. Memphis has a pretty short winter and we don't much like winter. But we pay for it in the spring and summertime heat.

As I mentioned, Jimmy had the three houses painted and the fumes made Rose wheeze a while. She settled down just about the time the heat got so bad that opening a couple of windows and letting the breeze blow all the way through the house didn't help. But we were out on the porch and it was hot and Layla was complaining she didn't feel good. So Jimmy after he had bought his car and had started thinking he could say all sorts of things about all sorts of things and be worth listening to said maybe we should all get in his Cadillac and turn on the air conditioner.

Heat will make you irritable even if you're nice. Layla was in a bad mood and didn't seem ready to put up with such stupidness. Not that Jimmy was stupid. Not at all. He was smarter than any of us in some ways and the only one of us who'd ever had a profession that included a uniform. But what she was going on about was that if you can buy a Cadillac with an air conditioner you can buy an air conditioner for a house.

So Jimmy said okay, he'd buy her an air conditioner.

"Now," is what Layla said instead of thank you. She wasn't feeling good at all. You could tell without her needing to say it and after a few sighs and some eye rolling she added, "Good God," and went inside, which I think embarrassed Jimmy a bit since he was left out there with me and Rose and neither of us said anything.

One thing about Jimmy, he can get a thing done. And by that afternoon he'd driven to the store and bought three window air conditioners, one for each house. And a white man in a Sears Service uniform was installing them for us.

And then I knew what it was to be rich. The air conditioner was in my and Rose's bedroom and I thought I might never want to leave that room again. I still felt bad about the way Jimmy got the money but I was comfortable for the first time in a while so I tried not to think about it.

When the Sears man turned on the air conditioner and said in his low way, "That oughta keep ya cool, ma'am," I could've hugged him. When he said "ma'am" it was completely different than with the wax-paper man. That first breeze across my belly gave me goose bumps and I stood in front of it for a few minutes until I worried that my cool stomach might make my baby uncomfortable.

And Rose seemed happier. She even asked me to make her some grits for dinner.

I worked on my raccoon for a while that night and was happier than I'd been in a long time just because of being cool and comfortable. I was getting close to finished. I had the skull arranged and the paws just about figured out. I could hardly wait to get it all glued down and hang it over my bed. And I could also hardly wait to put together Rose's stained-glass window. I knew I could get it finished before I had the baby and then the baby would be my project for a good while. All this to think about. All this world to think about. I was feeling that just about everything could stand being thought about and still there would be things you didn't know about it.

Air conditioning made it easier to think about this sort of thing. Otherwise you spend all your energy just trying to be comfortable in the heat. That was something to think about itself. That whole thoughts might not be thought just because the air wasn't cool enough.

But that got me to thinking about whether there might be some things you would think about in the heat that you wouldn't think about in a comfortable air-conditioned room.

The heat and the air conditioners kept us all inside more than usual and I didn't see Layla for more than a week. When I did see her I could tell she was bad sick. I was actually sort of shocked because her sickness wasn't taking its time like Rose's was, and to tell the truth she looked a lot like my mama did before she died.

In fact, at the same time Layla seemed to be having more wrong with her, I thought maybe Rose was getting a little bit better.

Muscadines

It's not just things like air conditioning that come from nowhere and make it easier to think, or harder. When I'm nauseated all I can think about is not throwing up. And I almost always pray more while I'm sick to my stomach because I feel like I will die, like I've never been well. Even though I know when I throw up after it's over I'll feel better, I am one of those people who will lie there and hope for anything to keep me from throwing up. I think it's the way one part of you takes over and it doesn't matter what's happening with other parts of you, your stomach is gonna throw up and that's all there is to it, even if you just threw up half an hour ago so that there is nothing to throw up so there's really no point in the whole thing. I hear that pushing out a baby has the same feeling, not being able to help it, but it's different because there is a point.

I had thrown up a couple of times and was feeling much better sitting out on the porch after being inside for so long, watching the train pass and feeling the rhythms of the train pour into my bones. I knew my baby had to feel the pounding shaking through the ground and up through the wood and through my body. I wondered if it could feel afraid while it was inside me but I figured probably not because when you are afraid, even a hug can make you feel better and if you think about it being inside somebody is like being hugged for nine months, which means everybody starts with something good, except for being born, which has to be a shock, all things told.

Jimmy came out on his porch and dragged out his black easy chair. Then he stepped across the little space that separated his porch from our porch and handed me a bowl of muscadines without saying anything. They were as cold as they can get without freezing and I took them like they were flowers but didn't say anything because I wasn't sure what he was up to by giving them to me. At the moment I hoped it was not something that would be complicated and make me have to say no to something that I wouldn't be sure about, but I also hoped it wasn't just asking me to hold his bowl of muscadines while he made himself comfortable in his black easy chair.

The first muscadines of the season taste like spring. By the time the train passed I had eaten half the bowl without trying to make clear with Jimmy why he had decided to give me something, which he hadn't done in a while. I wasn't eating fast but the train was long and I couldn't imagine what all it pulled inside.

When it was gone Jimmy asked me if he ought to take

Layla to a doctor now that he could afford it. I asked if Layla wanted to go to one and he said she said no. But he asked me if I would talk to her.

"You're a woman," he said before I could ask why he wanted me to talk with her. But me and Layla hardly ever talked. Whatever she thought about the world I couldn't even guess.

I kept eating muscadines and thinking about what I might say to her if I talked to her and forgetting my thoughts about Jimmy.

Then Jimmy asked me, "So how's that baby coming along?"

I didn't even answer, muscadines or no muscadines. That was exactly what I was worried about. I even thought about giving back the bowl and saying thank you to make things even and walking inside. Then I decided I was too happy to act that way and I knew this baby was gonna be all mine. "It's okay. It's coming along just fine, I guess," I said.

"It's something all right, growing a baby."

I knew he didn't anymore know what he was talking about. And to tell the truth I didn't want him to know. Not out of meanness or spite for Jimmy. But out of respect for me and my baby because it's a lot of work to understand a thing and I was doing the work and had been doing it for some time. You don't just ask after eight months how's that baby coming along, and you sure don't ask it when you started the whole thing and expect to get an answer that means a thing.

"It's coming along just fine" is all he got and all he wanted, I think.

Muscadines have a weak point so that when you bite them the whole wet glob of fruit comes popping through it. You push the skin with your tongue over to the side of your mouth. Then you push the fruit against the back of your teeth with your tongue and the seeds come out. Spit them out. Then chew the fruit. Then take the skin and work it open with your tongue. It's sort of bitter and sort of tangy but there is a soft thin sweet lining on the inside that you can suck on or scrape with your teeth.

Rose calls them scuppernongs. But that doesn't make as much sense as muscadine.

"All right," I said, "I'll try to talk to her. But she may as well be a China woman for all she's like me and likely to listen to anything I say."

He nodded and went on in to work. If you just work and don't do anything else I think you start to see the world different than somebody who sees it as magical or Catholic. I knew Jimmy was flat in the way he looked at the world. How's that baby coming along. What do you do with someone who has no more magic than that?

I looked down at the bowl. I have a strange thought when I eat muscadines that comes from the Bible and is sort of embarrassing. The story in the Bible where David collects the foreskins of the Philistines? Well, I always imagine a shoe box full of chewed muscadine skins.

The Eye

There are some things you just don't want other people to know. Like my idea about muscadines. That's not much to worry over but there are other things I wouldn't mention to other folks. I don't think I could. It seems like it might be wrong somehow for just anyone to know some things because not everyone knows how to know some things. At church the priests take confession and the idea seems to be that they know how to know things about you.

But by wrong I mean wrong not just because of some rule. Or a law. I mean wrong the way eating grass is wrong for a person. That's what I worried over about Layla. Once Jimmy got her on the computer it was like she was inside out. It was like trying to look inside a balloon to see what holds its shape but the air gets let out so it goes flat.

But while I was fretting over Layla Jimmy started getting worried about something besides Layla getting sick. It was so easy to read that man. I don't think he'd ever make it selling drugs or going into politics. I wouldn't tell him because

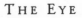

I am not a mean person but as smart as he was, and even though he had a profession and a uniform, he was simple about some things and some of the things he was simple about were some of the things that I think are more important than even stuff they write about in the newspapers or put on television and radio.

But finally I had to ask him what the problem was because he started looking at everybody who came by like they was gonna steal something. Layla was not fit to work and Jimmy started fretting all day and in a couple weeks I'd be Mama to somebody who had nothing to do with all this. Then Jimmy told me he was worried over maybe they were watching his computer site.

And trying to sound as disgusted as I could, not to be mean but to be truthful, I said lots of people must be watching judging by his car and the new paint and the air conditioners and the dresses and all. I said everybody could see her that wanted to without her being able to see them. It was like there was a big eyeball right in her window.

He said no, that he meant They were watching and he said with a capital T.

"Who is They?" I asked him. But he just shook his head like he was worrying over a sick baby and also like I didn't know anything about worrying, which was just pure wrong.

It took me another five minutes to get it out of him. It was that Ambrosia was sitting on the floor while Layla and her bums did things that people paid to watch. She wasn't watching, he said, like that made it okay. All she did was what she always does, rock and turn the pages of the book of colors. And he was right about that, though I wasn't about to agree with him. But now he was worried about being called a child pornographer. "You can go to jail for that," he said to make me see why he was fretting, "and people hate you for it."

Jimmy was not the jail type. Really, the type he was was a butcher who did good work and enjoyed his porch and told a few stories and sat with a kind of dull look on his face when women talked about babies or worried over the world. He was a plain man. He also wasn't the kind who you'd think would make a living putting people like Layla on the computer and he knew it, which was why once you got past the money he was as surprised as anybody I think at how things seemed to be turning out.

But I guess things look different on the computer than they do in real life, not that you could know that until you were on the computer and had something to compare to. The same as on TV or even in magazine pictures.

I didn't know how to help him. I just let him sit in his misery, not because I wanted to but because it was all I knew to do and he had dug the hole he was in so maybe there was something he was supposed to learn in the hole. It wasn't like I hadn't told him some things that might have kept him from digging it so deep, but like I said sometimes a thing needs to be lived to be understood instead of thought about or talked about. So maybe that's how it was with Jimmy. But one thing I did do was I started shooing away the men.

That was to help Layla because when you're weak it's like throwing up because you can't stand up for yourself and need somebody to help you.

Layla didn't have much to say to me about being so sick. Something about her eyes was already gone and I knew we'd never get her to a doctor. I thought to myself that in some ways the only difference between Layla and Ambrosia was that Layla had a gift for men. Like a machine. Or a Venus flytrap. Something alive that has to close around a thing that flies in except that with Layla it seemed the fly always got away and usually seemed better or at least the same. At least from the distance where I watched things. Watching from a distance is not the same as watching from outside. From outside things might look a lot different than the truth of the thing, which I suppose was Jimmy's big problem.

But I shooed them away. All the men.

And I thought about the way Jimmy talked about Them. The way They can check up on what you're doing on the computer. I was interested in the computer but that made me feel strange, like walking in on somebody looking in the drawer where you keep your underwear and such. I spent a long time thinking about how 'They' and 'the eye' seemed the same.

The Postcard

Like I said, when one thing changes everything changes. It wasn't just that Layla was sick and wouldn't have anything to do with a doctor, it was also that Rose seemed to start feeling better. She said, "Yslea, you can't get over old age the way you get over sickness. So there's nothing to get too happy about. But this warm weather has loosened up my joints. And that air conditioning keeps the warm weather from taking too much out of me. I'm feeling a little better."

So she took her medicine bottles one by one and put them back in the drawer of her little nightstand in the careful way she handled the few things she owned, against the day she started to feel sick again. She was still old and still tired. But what she had back for a little while was some feeling like she was part of the world again.

It wasn't too long before she went over to see Layla and she came back telling me we needed to think about where to bury her. When somebody who's old tells you that, you listen because you know they've thought about what death looks like and probably know better than anyone what the signs look like even if people are trying to hide them. I asked her if she told Layla and she said, "No, but she knows anyway."

And that was looking at a whole world of trouble not because of taking care of Layla when she was dead, the city could help with that, I guessed, but wondering what to do with Ambrosia. So me and Rose and Jimmy started talking about the problem headed down the road to us.

And that was when Jimmy started talking about this postcard he picked up somewhere. He showed us. It was a postcard at sunset on a beach in Mexico with two people lying back on beach chairs. "That's where I want to go," he said. And right after we'd just been talking about burying Layla and what to do with Ambrosia he started up again with how he was just gonna drive and drive. He'd sleep in his yellow Cadillac and he'd have all his stuff in the trunk and the backseat and the passenger side of the front. All his things would be around him inside the car he owned. He'd drive until he got to that beach in Mexico and then he'd buy a beach chair and he'd lie back and watch the sun go down with no worries.

Me and Rose didn't say anything right off because what do you say? But he kept bringing that postcard out to the porch like he wanted us to say how nice it was or something. Well, there was no chance I was gonna help him drive off into that Mexican sunset and leave us with Layla, who was perfectly fine before he came up with his big idea, on top of the fact of Ambrosia and my own baby. And Rose might be feeling better but she was right that you don't get over old age like you get over a sickness.

And what that meant was that before too long I would be by myself with a baby, Ambrosia, and Jesus. Pretty soon that was gonna be who we meant by "us."

"It's not fair for you to just up and go," I finally told Jimmy, and I knew I sounded scared. Maybe I hadn't made him feel any ties to the baby just about to push its way out into the world. But I never thought about everybody leaving all at the same time.

He just kept looking at that postcard like he wanted to jump into it. "I've never had the money to get myself out of here and now I do," he said. It was like it was the first time he knew he'd really go. Now that he had a whole lot of other things here to get out of like worrying over whatever it was he thought They were going to do, I saw that even my fear and the fact that I was right that it was not fair were just more things to get away from. It's like it's the opposite of love. I used to think the opposite of love was hate. But I was starting to think the opposite of love might be running away in the middle of things that ought to feel like they are yours.

And sure enough he didn't show up on the porch the next day. He was gone like he'd never been there. Flat gone. Which of course you can't do if you are connected to a baby by a cord. But maybe that's the difference between boys and girls, even though if boys understood more they would also feel connected since once a baby is out the connection doesn't have a cord, but it's still real. I hadn't let him be close, I know. But I still wanted to scream this at him. Everything had gotten just so hard and I was getting scared.

He left his door unlocked so I went on inside, even though I was scared, which is strange to me because I was scared by what wasn't there instead of by what was. Where his computer used to be he'd left an envelope with "Yslea" written on the front but spelled with an I, "Islea," with his lousy handwriting like he wrote it with one of those big pencils you get in first grade, which made me sad. There was five hundred dollars inside along with the postcard and the keys to the house.

So that got me to thinking why some people can just up and go and some people can't. Or maybe it's how you think about it, the difference between going and leaving. If you go, you go to somewhere. If you leave, you leave from somewhere. Both things'll get you out of the house but they are different as can be. I didn't have anyplace to go. And most everything would come with me anyway. The baby was part of my body and it felt like she would always be part of my body, which I can't leave until I die. And I didn't want to die, even though I was sad like I imagine an animal would feel waking up newborn in the dark among trees and alone.

It's Safer Standing on a Broken Track

Some things don't matter to some people. Things that might be the only reason other people live.

Now that I was thinking about what it was gonna be like to be alone I was thinking about all sorts of things.

Pay attention, just pay attention, was what I told myself. Some things that matter to a person will just sidle up next to her if she sits down and waits and pays attention. I did not used to know that. Not everything will act this way but some things will, a lot of what matters will. Like asking for a glass of water and finding a home. But whether a thing comes to you or you go to it, you have to pay attention or else you will miss the good thing that has come your way.

You have to pay attention to stay safe too. When you walk on the train tracks, even though you know how loud trains are you pay attention. You look back every now and then just to make sure a quiet one isn't sneaking up on you. That's why I like to walk on the old rusted track with grass growing up in it and the rotted wooden ties. The big nails have come out somehow and are scattered around and all orange with rust. A bum could sleep on this track and not worry. It's never gonna have another train passing over it.

So that track is given over to people, whoever happens to be passing by who doesn't want to walk on the tracks that the train might come down. I love to walk on the old tracks. Even when a train passes by on the good tracks I'm not afraid. I know I'm safe. The train is so tall, heavy, long, fast, carrying thousands of things that have nothing to do with me. I am afraid about other things that are more human-size, and I don't mind saying that anymore.

I didn't choose for Layla to die, or for Rose to die, or for Jimmy to leave. I didn't choose for Ambrosia to be rocking all the time, though she is manageable enough if she has her book. I can't even say I chose this baby except that when it was growing inside me it felt as natural as an elbow.

I could spend the better part of a day thinking about things I didn't choose. How perfectly laid out the raccoon was. All the ideas that come to me when I let them, when I'm not afraid of them. About the only thing I choose some days is to be quiet. The kind of being quiet that I usually choose is meandering on the broken track, taking account of things my size.

I'm content with that. And that kind of contentment makes it easier to talk to folks I might not talk to so easy otherwise. White folks. Or police. It's the kind of peace that lets me say you're welcome when someone says thank you instead of just saying thank you back, which never made sense to me, even though I do it sometimes like it isn't okay for me to have thank you said to me.

So when the white police came on up to where I was sitting on the porch in the afternoon, wiping my face and thinking, my heart stayed as calm as calm could be.

They asked me where Jimmy was and could they see his house and his computer. They wore suits but they had badges on their belts and they were some serious people.

They wanted to know could they talk to Layla. I said no, she was dying. But when they said if they didn't talk to her everybody could be in even more trouble, I asked Layla and she talked to them.

Ambrosia came out on the porch while they were looking around Jimmy's house. They looked at her and didn't say much past thank you when they left. I said you're welcome but they were already around the corner. Even though I stayed calm while they were there, when they left I noticed that I did feel shaken up even with them gone and even though I had not done anything wrong that I knew of.

Peripheral Vision

I woke up early and somehow before I'd even thought about it, like the idea was just sitting there waiting for me to wake up to have it, I knew what I needed to do that day. I cleaned Jimmy's house. I made sure all the dishes were washed. I cleaned the sheets and made up the bed with no wrinkles, the place where my baby first started to grow. I threw out the almost empty box of cereal and the cookies that were all he had in his cabinet, and I threw out the half carton of chocolate milk he had in his refrigerator. It was the kind of kitchen a ten-year-old boy would have, not a grown-up. I washed his towels and swept everywhere. I dusted with a damp cloth, then I made sure the front door and the back door were both locked along with all the windows. Then I put the key in a little box and felt like something was finished. And that was a real good feeling.

Then I sat down and put the last few little bones on my raccoon and I hung it up. Then without even standing back and looking at it long, without thinking much about what it felt like to finish it and have no leftover pieces except a few bone crumbs that came off in the box and weren't really pieces, I sat down with my heart set on making the stained-glass window for Rose. I had the square piece of plastic and the box full of pieces of glass in all sorts of colors. Each piece I looked at made me think of how Jimmy, even though he did some things to be ashamed of, also every now and then did something that nobody could do unless he had some goodness in him.

I glued the red one in the middle. That was the only thing I knew had to be. Where the rest went just sort of came to me. It was different than the raccoon. Different in a lot of ways.

It took me maybe four hours to be happy with how everything was arranged and to glue the pieces down. Then another hour to make sure it was dry. And when I hung it up in the window there was still enough sunlight for Rose to see it.

"Oh, Yslea," she said, and I felt good. "Did you know," she said, "that the doctor once told me I've lost most of my peripheral vision? I'd never heard of peripheral vision and didn't even know I had it until he told me it was gone since it went away so slowly. I can only see things straight in front of my eyes. The vision I've got left is just about big enough for your window there to fit in. Thank you, child."

"You're welcome."

And that was another thing finished.

So I went outside and sat on the sofa and thought about how a thing gets finished, which is one of those things that doesn't seem hard to say unless you have to say it to yourself or somebody else. The way a thing gets finished is not always because you know where you want to go, what it'll look like when it's done, but sometimes it's just being ready to see that it is done when it's done and then to call it done. Not everybody can do that last part, and even somebody who can do it can't do it every time and be sure. That much I've learned.

When Rose told me she'd lost her peripheral vision I started paying attention to peripheral vision. It's different from what's in front of you. What's in front of you is just there. You can think about it all at once. But what is in your peripheral vision is not so clear. First you think you're looking with your peripheral vision and nothing changes except that you notice something else on the other side of your peripheral vision. Your eyes have not even moved.

So I tried to look with all my peripheral vision at the same time. It's not as easy as it sounds. Then I tried to look with all my vision at one time. And I tried to let everything be a thing. The track, Jesus, the fence, the bum standing there staring, the trees lopped into Ys, everything. But that was too much to do all at the same time.

Maybe I should just practice is what I thought at first.

And I did for a little bit. Then it started to seem sort of a waste of time, even though I didn't have a whole lot else to do. It seemed like I was just making stuff up. So I thought about making up the way I put the glass on the stained-glass window. I thought it was beautiful but how could I know?

I started to feel not as happy, just a little bit, but it mattered. And I asked myself why. And I answered myself and knew I was right. It's that it can be a frightening thing to be the one making something up. It might look solid and finished to someone else but you always know you are the one who made it. It can make you have doubts. Like maybe it isn't good enough. Maybe you're not good enough.

A Darkness That Can Be Felt

Of course the way things are, just about the time things start seeming clear and good an attack of darkness comes on. And the Lord knows the same thing. God no sooner announced from heaven that this is my Son, the Beloved, with whom I am well pleased than the same Beloved was led up by the spirit into the wilderness to be tempted by the devil.

It's not the kind of thing that would ever happen to Robinson Crusoe. It's a darkness on the inside like the darkness God had Moses spread over Egypt. That's what sticks in my chest somewhere. What I've heard over and over through the years is the Lord said to Moses, "Stretch out your hand toward heaven so that there may be a darkness over the land of Egypt, a darkness that can be felt."

Thank God it doesn't happen more often.

So I went from the calm evening thinking about peripheral vision to lying in my bed that night knowing Jimmy was gone and Layla was dying and Rose was dying and I started to be afraid. It comes on slow the same way night creeps by slow. Sometimes you think of things like the things I've mentioned but then other things come on in. You might think of a worm trying to cross a sidewalk in summertime and how it doesn't stand a chance, or how if I hadn't met Jimmy the baby wouldn't be inside me. Even if I'd met Jimmy some other day or some other minute then maybe everything would be different. Then you seem alone.

Then it's just feeling afraid without even having a name for it or seeing anything in your mind that makes you afraid. That's the darkness that is so dark even the light in your mind is dark and you wonder if you can even dream anymore.

What I wanted was for my baby to be okay. What I wanted was a place to stay. I wanted my peace.

But in the darkness funny things can happen. Out of nowhere you start thinking things like whether Layla was just dying from her own darkness or whether it was some bad disease you could catch. It was like the insides of her were going away, just disappearing, and it didn't take more than a few weeks to get that way. You could see the curves of her breasts whistling down like untied water balloons lying in the grass. You could see her skinny legs, which just a little while ago looked made by God to squeeze unhappy men until they groaned with pleasure to be let go. It would have been so easy to put a pillow over her face to make the pain in our houses go away.

When the darkness comes thoughts just go crazy. All the things I thought about the raccoon started to seem made up. All the things at church started to seem like the kinds of things you could make up too. Stories about Egypt and golden calves. Manna, water from the rock, the valley of dry bones. Even angels and the Body of Christ.

Rose was over there snoring when the darkness came. I listened to it and was afraid. It sounded a little like all the drunk burnt-out grown-ups in the crack house snoring through the morning after a night that was too much for a body. Only Rose was a different kind of grown-up. Even though she pulled out medicine bottles when she felt sick she was not afraid of dying, and when she said it you knew she meant it. And when I asked why she said it was because we only have love to look forward to. I didn't ask her how she knew this but I sure was glad that was the reason she wasn't afraid of death instead of it being something like just wanting to leave this world.

Then I started to think, okay, that old woman is a good woman. A real good woman. And then I knew I was past the worst part of the darkness. And I remembered that there's nothing in church that says you won't feel pain and loss. And that is true. There's a lot in this world that's not a lie. I figured nobody could believe that everything is a lie and still get much of anything done that matters. By the time I figured all this out the darkness wasn't so dark anymore and I had hold of goodness and I had hold of truth. With that I relaxed enough to get a couple of hours of sleep before the sun came up and I had to work out what I was gonna do with the fact that I made it through the night.

Revisiting the Troll

Almost nothing is as scary in the daytime as it is at night. But the darkness didn't go away for good the next morning. It just quieted down some and had better manners in the daytime. I didn't know but that it maybe never goes away. I thought that if that's so it would have to be tamed just like every other sadness. Otherwise you can't get on with what needs to be done. When something is a part of the world it doesn't do any good to complain if only because of how much energy it takes to complain when it ain't changing anything. I guess we have to let the darkness live right alongside everything else and take its turn.

I was cooking grits for Rose, thinking about the night, and I was tired. Just tired. I wanted just for a little while for somebody I could trust who was stronger than me to watch over things while I slept and then when I was awake to help me figure out how I was gonna get settled in my body and get ready to have my baby.

But I couldn't stop thinking of Layla. I had never seen

her happy. Even though I couldn't do much for her myself I thought of something that might make her feel better for a little because I knew she knew darkness.

I could hardly wait to get the grits done to get on with my idea. There was no telling when my big ripe body was gonna open up. And there was no telling when Layla's body was gonna be too scrawny to stay alive. I had to move if I was gonna get my idea done before it was too late.

When I brought Rose the grits she was staring up at the stained-glass window. That made me feel good. I told her I had some things to do and she said she would just rest after she ate.

I got a plastic Coke bottle and filled it with water and made two white-bread-and-bologna sandwiches and then I started walking. I walked on down the track, then over to the road, then to the Bare Sticks Bridge. I was so big I had to be careful stepping down the steep hill with all the gravel and loose dirt. I got up under the bridge and my hips were aching like the bones were coming loose.

Sure enough the Troll was up in the angle between the bridge and the earth where he lived. And he was grunting and grunting and watching me. I could tell he knew who I was. It was like he was grunting so he wouldn't say, "Give us some of that," over and over, which if he was doing that because he saw that it bothered me was very kind of him. Watching him trying not to say, "Give us some of that," was like watching someone trying not to cough.

He was crouched like what a praying mantis looks like

and was watching me and grunting and waiting to see what it was I wanted.

I told him that for sure Layla was dying and somebody should know.

I couldn't have said why I thought he was one of the ones to know and it was hard to guess what he heard or understood. I didn't try to think up anything else to say to him. But I didn't feel scared like the last time.

I laid down one of my sandwiches in a baggie on the ground for him and got on out of there so I could walk on and tell whoever I saw so people would know. If you're like Layla and you're dying, it's not right that nobody knows and you'd die without even the comfort of knowing you'd be remembered.

The Troll scurried after me and stuck his nasty head up and looked after me while I walked away.

I told him to tell everybody he saw. He sort of nodded, I couldn't tell. Then he scurried back under the bridge. I expect he didn't see a lot of people.

The rest of the day I walked up the tracks and back. I must have seen twenty men I recognized and I told them the same. That Layla was dying. Since I needed to keep moving before I wore out I didn't stop and chat or find out what any of them thought about what I was telling them, but every one of them either nodded or stared in a way like they were sad and couldn't even bring themselves to nod. I wished Layla could see that.

I ate my other sandwich and I drank my water. And

when I was so tired I could barely stand it and my hips were aching so much, I walked on back home and lay down and fell asleep with no fear, full of a tired and delicious emptiness.

Black Man on a White Sand Dune

I had fallen asleep while it was still daylight.

When I woke up it was night. There was a faint blue light sort of like moonlight coming from the streetlamp near my window and I lay there very still and felt the slightest movement from my quiet baby. I let my eyes roll back just a little bit and I saw the ghost-colored skeleton of my raccoon mounted on the board and reminding me of all sorts of order. I saw the black outline of beautiful old Rose curved under her cover. I saw the gray-blue ears of Jesus the donkey sticking up by the window where he stood. And above his head was my stained-glass window.

I could hear Rose breathe.

I could just barely hear a jet flying over and then a little bit later a helicopter, machines of the air in a world I almost never think of, know nothing about except for what I learned in the book I had as a child and the magazines at the magazine rack.

I closed my eyes and then opened them again.

I started thinking about all the deformed or injured people I had known in my life. I had seen lots of people with too much sugar in their blood who'd had their legs cut off. I had once accidentally walked into the bathroom and seen a man who'd had cancer in a gland and had his privates cut off. He seemed to need to explain that to me later when I said I was sorry for walking in and he said he was the one sorry and he looked at me like I was a little girl, which I was, but he didn't know what all I'd seen, and I said for what and he looked at me looking him in the eye and he said he didn't know exactly. Then he laughed and then he hugged me not in a nasty way but like I imagine a grandpa would hug and said thank you. So I smiled and said, "For what?" and he laughed even more and said he didn't know that either but thanks for that too and that we'd better stop or we'd be there all night. It was one of the first times I felt like I had made somebody feel better, even though I did not know how or why.

I'd seen men who'd been in war and had their arms cut off. I'd seen young men with their faces cut in fights and thick scars growing up like tumors on their boyish beautiful skin. I'd seen women so big they could barely put one foot in front of the other. I'd seen women like my mama waste into a sack of bones. I'd heard old men cough all night until I thought they'd cough their lungs out. I'd seen a man take crack and start having a seizure and that day was the last time he said a word you could understand, the last day he used a toilet. After that I used to pass him and he'd be slumped over in his wheelchair on his front porch where his half-sister took care of him. He just stared past me and drooled. He was gone. He was the scariest man I knew. But he was only twenty-something when that happened, not much older than me now.

I'd seen just about everything.

I closed my eyes on Rose, Jesus, the raccoon, the window.

Then in my mind, and not even meaning to, I saw the man I wanted to meet. I didn't know why I wanted to meet him except that he was strong and also happy.

He was very black and the muscles of his face dimpled when he smiled and showed his great white teeth. His nose was strong and full like he could breathe the whole world in for joy. His clothes were clean and his hat was made of woven cloth.

In my mind he stood on a white sand dune with one foot slightly higher up the dune than the other. I have never seen a sand dune except in magazines so it surprised me. He was looking down to where the palm trees leaned toward the blue water.

I said, "Hello."

He smiled and he said, "My dear girl."

That was all. I couldn't say if he sounded French, Jamaican, African, Northern, or Southern. His eyes laughed for joy at the sight of my big belly. I could tell he knew history and was not the kind of man who was unmoved by sadness. But he seemed to breathe it all in and then breathe it all out. I wanted him to pick me up and put me on his shoulders and walk me around to give me a little more time to grow up.

And then I all of a sudden knew I could be like him. I knew it. I saw him so clearly.

I opened my eyes. Rose, Jesus, the raccoon. I knew how to love. That much I knew. I figured I had just seen my guardian angel.

A Chorus of Hoboes, Bums, and Whores

I slept longer than I usually do. I knew my body knew what it needed to get ready to let go of the baby so I didn't feel like any of the day was wasted even if I slept.

Rose was still sleeping. I figured her body was doing the same, taking what it needed to get ready to die.

That made me think of my guardian angel. And I thought maybe he was looking over the whole row, all five of us, counting the baby, like I didn't have to worry anymore if Jesus was white or black, coming soon or coming later.

Then I heard it. At first I thought a group of folks must be crying or wailing and since I was devoted to giving Layla the gift of shooing men away since she was too weak to do it I almost pulled myself up and went out to take care of it. But I listened for a minute or so. And it wasn't crying. There was a tune of sorts. But the window was closed and the air conditioner hummed too loud for me to hear what was going on.

I got up and wrapped myself in a blanket and walked out onto the porch. And there in the yard standing in the dust and weeds inside the chicken-wire fence were twenty or thirty people, mostly men but a few women too who I had never seen before. But I recognized most of the men. The Troll was there in front with his hands behind his back. Their clothes were all rags. Their hair was dirty as could be. I didn't see any of the men in suits who'd come once they'd found Layla on the computer. Just the folks I suspect the Troll knew and a handful of folks I'd talked to.

I sat down on my sofa and pulled my blanket around me and listened in wonder. I knew the train would be coming soon so I hoped they got their singing done before that. Layla's window was open a little like it always was but she and Ambrosia were inside. They were singing Christmas carols. I guess that was all everybody knew from when they were children so that's what they were singing. "Silent Night, Holy Night." And then "Jingle Bells." Then they sang one verse of "Twinkle Twinkle Little Star," which didn't make any sense to me but they seemed to mean it so I kept listening and listening.

I watched them. None of them knew all the words but about the time one of them stumbled over something, another one happened to know those words so all together they got through the songs.

Just then I heard the whistle of the train and knew they had about five minutes before everything was swallowed up by a roar. Even though maybe it seems like it ought to have, their singing wasn't gonna stop the train.

They ran out of songs they all knew so they started singing "Silent Night" again and it was better the second time through.

I kept wishing Layla would come to the door and at least give them a little wave. But for all I knew she had died in the night. Though I suspected Ambrosia might come out when her mama wasn't there anymore and float like a balloon some child had let loose.

The train rolled in right over the last verse of "Silent Night." I could see their mouths still moving. I guess they wanted to finish the song. Then for a bit they all stood around. No one could talk because of the train and we had all seen that four engines pulled it so it would go on forever.

Then the Troll who had his hands behind his back must have decided that Layla wasn't coming out and he had best do what they had come to do. So he pulled out a yellow kite and as the representative of the group he brought it up to her door and laid it on the porch. I could see his mouth moving and I figured he was mumbling his usual but maybe I didn't understand what he meant by his little phrase, like it might have been a prayer or a way to wish her good things while she suffered so.

The wind from the train blew the smell of the men toward me and with the baby up against my stomach I almost threw up. But they were like a little respectful congregation with the Troll as the priest. So I let them be and I sat feeling grateful to somebody for letting me see them do this thing.

With all the racket from the train and with the kite delivered and the songs sung, pretty soon they scattered. And soon the yard was empty except for Jesus coming around the corner and the wind from the train cleared the smell of the homeless men. And then it was just me. And Jesus.

Layla Flies a Kite

When the train finally passed there was still a hot wind blowing down the tracks.

I wasn't in any hurry to move. My hips hurt. My belly was stretched as far as it could stretch. My breasts were bigger than I ever thought they could be. I felt ripe as a honeydew melon, full of milk, water, and blood. Even though I hurt I was content.

Just then Layla's door opened. Ambrosia walked out and stepped on the kite like it wasn't there. She sat as usual, rocking, looking at her book.

The door was open and everything was quiet for a good while. But I was in the mood to wait.

Then Layla's hand reached out like a bone and took hold of the yellow kite. She stepped out. I wasn't ready for that, God have mercy. She must not have eaten a bite for three weeks, all shriveled up and sick-looking like an old woman, Christ have mercy. I can't prove it but I still couldn't help but think it was the wax-paper man that made her sick.

She held the kite like she'd hold a little girl's dress wishing she could buy it. "Ambrosia, you want to fly it?" she said for some reason. Of course Ambrosia may as well have been on the other side of the tracks. It made me especially sad to watch, even though I've seen the same sort of thing over and over. But Layla didn't ask it like she was mad at anyone, like she usually did, which was scary to see because she asked it like Ambrosia might be interested, almost not remembering exactly who Ambrosia was.

Then Layla looked at me. But it wasn't like she was looking at me. It was like she was using her body to look at me, like she wasn't all of a piece anymore, like her body was a puppet with a little string to make her eyes blink.

There was a frog screaming out in some puddle of stagnant water. I suppose that caught her attention for a moment and she looked away but then she looked back at me.

"Will you help me fly it?" she asked, the first thing she ever asked me to do.

So I pushed myself up off the sofa and took the kite. She sat down and held the string with both hands like a little girl and waited with a grin on her face that was also scary because of how bony her face was. But I reminded myself that this was still just Layla, just like I had reminded myself with my own mama when she died and just like I hope somebody will be good to me when it is my time to die. I pulled the kite out to the tracks where the hot wind blew like a gift and grabbed the kite and carried it on up to the sky.

I came back into the yard and stood there with my hands

on my aching hips looking up at the yellow kite and the white clouds and the blue sky. I hoped the bums all over the place would see it like the star of Bethlehem and know that they did something good. Layla and her bums was like Ambrosia and her book of colors. It was a whole world other than my world.

I looked back over to the porch. Layla was sort of rocking, just slightly, almost with the same rhythm as Ambrosia. Her head was tilted up just slightly and she closed her eyes and felt the sun for a little bit. Then she looked at me and I knew that I was gonna be taking care of Ambrosia. I smiled at the thought even though it would be hard.

Then Layla opened up her fingers and the last of the string flew out and left her hands empty.

If I could paint sadness I'd paint Layla. I don't know who she was. But she stood up and just barely, lightly like a butterfly, kissed Ambrosia's head and went on inside and died. It was the thing most like a fairy tale I've ever seen.

"Ambrosia," I said, "you want to come inside for some lemonade?"

She didn't answer or look at me but when I went on inside she jumped up and stood at the door rocking. She liked lemonade. I brought her a glass full and she drank it down.

I didn't know what I was gonna do with her right then. I didn't know what to do. So I decided to do nothing. I'd just let her be. I had to.

Piedmont and Son

I don't know how Mr. Piedmont found out Layla was dead, but I was glad he did. It was maybe a few hours after I found her and called the police.

Mr. Piedmont knew how to take care of things. The hearse wasn't an old sad-looking black Cadillac station wagon. First off, it was white, clean and shiny. The wheels were classy. It looked like something you might want to ride in even if you weren't dead.

Through the kitchen window I saw Mr. Piedmont drive up and get out. But I didn't go to the door until he knocked.

He was a big man and filled up the whole doorway. And as big as he was from a distance, when he looked at me and smiled he felt even bigger, like I was the size of a child. I imagine there were kings somewhere in his history.

"I'm here to help Miss Layla." He handed me a business card. "Piedmont and Son" was written in silver, in cursive. It was the first business card anybody had given me. I kept it.

"I can't—"

"All the fees are taken care of," he said in a way that said don't be embarrassed about that.

"I should tell the priest."

"He's on his way."

Mr. Piedmont was a man large enough to take care of death. With his black suit and his pressed white shirt, his golden tie and his bald head, he was one to go back and forth between the living and the dead.

So I took him on over to Layla's house. He stepped in and looked around with a certain respect. Then he took out his glasses and put them on and that made me feel even safer for some reason, the way he looked like he knew so much and knew the right things. He walked around the bed and adjusted the sheet on Layla.

"My son will be here soon and we will take care of everything."

"Thank you, Mr. Piedmont."

"It will be another day before the funeral."

I nodded but I think he saw on my face that I didn't want to watch her being buried. I looked at the big man to see if he was going to say something that would feel like he was chastising me. But of course he did not. I was not his concern just then, for one thing, and for another he was a good man.

Then I asked for no particular reason, "Do you like your job, Mr. Piedmont?"

He looked at me full of confidence. "It is a calling, ma'am, more than a job."

"I imagine that's true."

For just a moment I felt my calmness and I felt around for fear and didn't find any. Part of it had to do with Mr. Piedmont. Part of it had to do with me. Just then I wished I had a calling and just as sudden knew that I did.

There were things to do so I excused myself and left Mr. Piedmont to tend to his own calling while I tended to mine. Just as I was about to walk out the door Mr. Piedmont's son came in followed by the priest.

Mr. Piedmont's son was a beautiful man. He was as tall as Mr. Piedmont but skinnier. Dressed in the same black as his father, same pressed white shirt, same golden tie. He was calm and serious in a way I think Jimmy could have been but wasn't. I think it was that his business was the place where all the talk about being equal actually happens. It's like if you've looked at death enough times you can't help but understand some things, and once you understand those things what else can life do to make you afraid?

The three men took care of that part of life while I washed the dishes at Rose's. I saw them take Layla out covered with a royal red velvet cover, which I thought was a nice touch that Layla would have liked. I watched them. I watched Mr. Piedmont's son. He was a fine man, I could tell.

Then he turned and came back to my door and knocked.

"We'll be leaving now, ma'am."

"Yslea, sir." And then I felt silly calling him sir, not that he didn't deserve it.

He smiled with the same comforting smile his daddy had. He had been raised so well, I thought, which is the kind of thing I notice these days now that I will be raising somebody. He handed me his business card just like his father's.

"Thank you," I said. I kept his card too.

Under the House

Now Jimmy was gone and Layla was gone. About this time I started wishing I had thought more about what might happen to Ambrosia. Not in general like I had been thinking but in the everyday details since you live life in details and not in general. This was not about a theory of time or what makes a thing beautiful. This was about a strange girl who I could not even tell if she knew her mother was dead. This was a practical question, not one I could solve lying on my bed staring at my raccoon for inspiration. This question had to be solved while doing a practical thing. So I went over to Layla's place and started to clean up.

To tell the truth Layla was a perfectly fine housekeeper. So there wasn't much to do. The only mess I found was boxes of cereal with the tops ripped off and oatmeal and empty cookie packages, which explained why anytime I left out a sandwich to see if she wanted it Ambrosia only ate a couple of bites. And even that mess was shoved into a corner of the pantry, like Ambrosia picked up a habit from her mama of being neat as best she could. Even with Layla so sick the last few weeks all the dishes were washed and put away, the sink was clean, her bathroom was neat without even the little pieces of hair that break off, which I leave in the bathroom all the time. I don't think Jimmy wiped the dust off anything but his computer the whole time he lived in his house, but when I ran a rag over Layla's windowsills there was nothing on them except a few books lined up alphabetically.

I noticed that when Piedmont and Son took Layla's poor old skinny body with them, they made up her bed instead of leaving it rumpled. They sure were quality folks.

I never would rummage through anybody's stuff while they were still alive but I wondered if it was okay when they're dead. Somehow being dead seems to change a lot of things. But not everything. If it is wrong to badmouth a person while they are alive it's still wrong when they are dead, in my view.

So I decided not to rummage but instead just to look closely at things while I cleaned and set aside what seemed like it would be useful to Ambrosia.

Layla had a little shrine to the Blessed Virgin Mary on her dresser. Maybe it was something about her having ancestors from Louisiana or Haiti or someplace but she had a lot of religion in her. She and I never talked about it but I was thankful that I followed her to the Catholic church and while she was sick I prayed for her at the altar, and when it didn't work and she died anyway I figured I would start lighting a candle every now and then for her and thinking about where she might be. Purgatory? Heaven? I knew it wasn't hell. She had the names of her bums written on little pieces of paper and piled up in front of the Virgin Mary. I suspect it would be hard to send her to hell with a good conscience.

I was standing there looking at Mary holding the naked baby Jesus and thinking about how much I looked forward to holding and loving my baby when I heard a thump like out of a fairy tale right up under my feet that scared me. At first I thought could that be the rattlesnake striking at this or that, a mouse or a rat maybe? But then it happened again. Then again.

I went outside and looked up under the house and there was Ambrosia lying in that nasty dirt kicking the ground with her feet.

"Ambrosia, what are you doing under there?" But she didn't even look at me. "Ambrosia, you are gonna get bit by the rattlesnake and don't you come running to me." That is the strangest child I have ever seen. But then I knew that she knew her mama was dead.

Well, I wasn't gonna crouch there long with eight and a half months of baby hanging off my belly so I went on inside and called the fire department.

They came out and crawled up under the house. They had to chase her from Layla's house to Jimmy's house to ours but they finally got her out. She went to the corner of the yard, miserable, and rocked herself while Jesus sort of hung his head and seemed to wonder what to do.

The fire department had been all up under the houses so I asked them if they saw a rattlesnake missing his rattle. They said no. So he was probably long gone.

The place was starting to feel mighty empty.

The Investigation

I felt so bad for Ambrosia sitting in the corner of the yard not understanding where her mama had gone. Maybe it's easier for someone like her to lose her mama since she never paid much attention to Layla in the first place, not that she could help it. What I mean is that I don't know how she felt pain. Thinking of Ambrosia losing her mama is like thinking of a fish breathing air. You know it hurts but you don't know how exactly.

But I didn't want to mess with her because she had a way of living her life that was all of a piece and that didn't like to be interrupted. I was thanking the Lord the fire department had chased her out from under the house and had eased my mind about the rattlesnake.

But not much after they left somebody from the Department of Family and Children Services came by and knocked on the door and the second the first sentence came out of the lady's mouth I felt like a criminal for even caring about the girl.

Lord have mercy on Ambrosia's soul. They came with a policeman. The policeman went out to Ambrosia and stood around like he didn't know what to do with the strange girl, which he didn't.

When somebody comes into your house like that it makes everything that is familiar that you live with seem like underwear on a clothesline. They let their eyes wander over things without even trying to hide the fact that they're looking at your stuff, not in a curious way, which anyone can be, but to see if you measure up. Measure up to what? I wanted to know as my brain chattered like crazy, which happens when I'm mad. Measure up to whatever they think measuring up looks like, I figured, because there wasn't any rule book from God they had a hold of, I was pretty sure. I just wanted them to leave before they even told me why they were there.

But this woman with a narrow nose, all dressed in a business suit and acting like she had to save the world from me, pulled a file folder out of her cheap briefcase and opened it up. Do you know this man? Do you know this woman? Did you ever see so-and-so visit? And so on. I was so mad I could have called her a name or two. She wouldn't even listen to me when she asked me a question so I wanted to say what is the point of asking me a question if you are not gonna listen to the answer, but I didn't because that kind of person will take every little thing and use it to make things worse.

She pulled out picture after picture copied off the computer. First Layla with this bum and then with that bum, parts of Layla and the bums marked out with permanent ink for decency, I guess. And at the foot of the bed was Ambrosia with her book of colors.

Yes, I knew Layla, she's dead. Yes, I knew Jimmy, he's gone I don't know where. No, Layla did not tell me her plans for Ambrosia. I think she was just gonna let the girl stay here with me.

Why isn't that possible? What makes it okay for you to take her when you don't know her, then put her in some foster home where people don't know her? Not one thing about her. I know her. She's special and she needs things to be a certain way and it takes time to understand.

A course? I have to go to school to learn how to take care of Ambrosia now her mama is dead? What are you all thinking? Tell me one thing in that course that will help me take care of a girl like Ambrosia?

But he's gone. I had nothing to do with that computer. I did not agree with what he was doing and I told him so to his face.

But before the computer it was different. It was just the way Layla was. It might have been bad but in a way that was almost good, I think.

But it didn't matter what I said to the lady from the government. She was hell-bent on saving the girl from me. And since she had a policeman with her she could do whatever she wanted and she knew it.

It was rare that I heard Ambrosia scream like I heard her scream when they took her off to somewhere to protect her from me. But I understand evil. I had enough grown men look at me in the crack house from the time I was six. I know evil. And what they were doing was evil, evil, evil.

The Book of Colors

All my life that I can remember I have felt like I'm called to by things that other folks think just look like things sitting there. It might be the sign that Jesus is coming soon, or the raccoon, or Paris, France, or a rattlesnake, or pieces of glass. But everything else is sort of gray, which is how regular work gets done. The thinking is gray, the seeing is gray. You don't feel afraid of anything but you also don't hope for anything.

Then all of sudden a window goes up and there is a color that calls out from the gray. Green, black, red, white, gold. It comes with a shape and a meaning. Snake, medicine bottle, raccoon skeleton, Paris, France, the face of my guardian angel. I collect these memories like a boy picking up the treasure of pebbles, bottle caps, and batteries.

But right after the evil black woman and policeman took Ambrosia away all the gray washed over me. I was hot, dead tired, and empty. My sleepy baby rolled a shoulder, then went back to being still. Even though my body was more full than it had ever been, the skin on my belly stretched as far as it would go, everything full, full, full, even so I still felt empty like I had just cried for hours and thrown up. Even emptier.

A bum walked down the tracks with his greasy backpack and his tangled beard. He didn't even look over. He was just staring down counting ties or something. And he moved on. He seemed more like a tangled bush, the roots of a bush, more like something all from the earth than a man. I had never seen him before and he passed on and it was like a slow version of the train driver passing by, just a face with no details to make it particular. But that was the grayness. Gray everywhere.

And then a window popped open. A little fleck of color made my eye stop roaming over the diamonds in the chicken-wire fence. Down in the corner of the box that was our yard. The book of colors.

I didn't know if she had shoved it there or dropped it.

But after all we'd been through as grown-ups with Ambrosia ignoring all of it except her book, that little book of colors would not let go of my eye. It was sharp. It was barbed, a fishhook in my mind.

I got up and got the book, the size of my hand, just those few colored cardboard pages stapled together. The edges were worn and dingy from Ambrosia turning them back and forth.

I turned the pages. Green, black, red, white, gold.

What did Ambrosia see? There were no words, no pictures, just colors. I had watched her turn these pages a thousand times, always at the same speed it seemed to me, slow, never speeding up or slowing down, like a streetlight changes colors at the same speed hour after hour after hour. I never watched for a pattern. But maybe there was one, like the streetlight. I thought it was important for me to try to see what this book did to keep Ambrosia from flying to pieces.

I remembered being a little girl and grown-ups who I didn't understand and who scared me would step over me while I lay down on the floor looking down through the heating grate and it was a whole other world down there, safe, where things collected along with dust, and the part I could see was like the first part of a path that disappears into a forest. The duct went to some mysterious place far away and there was the sound like breathing or a cave and I could hum and hear it rumble into the other world. "Get up off that floor," somebody would say but then they would just walk over me. They didn't see it. They didn't see that I had my mind and heart down there where no one else ever looked. The same with my Great Book of World Transportation. They didn't know the meaning of what I was looking at.

I couldn't say what the book of colors did for Ambrosia. I couldn't say why the colors helped her. Maybe it was how God talked to her.

As sure as Jimmy was gone and Layla was dead I knew if

I didn't get Ambrosia back and give her the book of colors, she would die. I thought what it would be like if all my ideas went away and I never had another real thought. I would go crazy. Take away my ideas from me and I would go crazy. So I thought maybe I would call Mr. Piedmont's son and ask if he could help me.

Birth in the Chapel

I had no sooner hung up with Mr. Piedmont's son, happy that he was gonna help me, than that baby went from just lying around for eight and a half months to kicking up the most god-awful storm inside my belly. My water broke and before long I was feeling like I had to push as much as I had to breathe. This was another one of those places where it didn't do any good to say don't push because I didn't have any choice in the matter. My body was gonna do what it had to do and there wasn't much I could do about it, though I preferred not to have the baby in the kitchen.

I had only known one person well who had a baby, my friend from ninth grade, and it took twelve hours of pushing to get her baby out. I thought I might be lucky if I only pushed twelve minutes the way it felt. I held on to the kitchen table and breathed.

Rose had called out to me for months and months and I never minded. I was always there even when it was just she wanted to know I was there just in case.

"Rose," I yelled, although I tried to just say it so I didn't scare her.

She wasn't scared, though. "Come in here, child," she called out right away. She seemed to know right off what was happening and what to do. When I got into the bedroom she was sitting on the side of her bed. She reached over to her side table and put on her hairnet, which she never wore. "Come on over here, Yslea, and let's take a look."

"You ever done this?"

"Used to be this was the only way it happened. Truth is I don't do a whole lot except try not to drop the baby. All the work is yours."

I don't know what to say about Rose. She gave me a fine gift. She found something inside her and used it all to help me. And she knew what she was doing. She put her fingers inside me. No more than half an hour passed but she said, "Get ready to see your baby, Yslea. Now, you just do what your body says and I'll get some things ready for the baby."

She reached into her medicine drawer and pulled out some alcohol. She had scissors, shoe string, a couple of blankets. She shuffled around and every now and then put her fingers inside me and said, "Lord, this baby is coming fast. And in the middle of the day when everybody is well rested, glory be to God."

But I could hardly listen to her. I was looking up at the stained-glass window with the red eye in the middle and the colors around it just like I liked them.

For the time being I saw my body was no more my own while delivering that baby than it would be my own when I died. All I could do was watch it. And I felt like I was nothing but the pain of my body but when I look back on it, it makes me wonder if I am even the same thing as my body. When you die or have a baby it sure feels like it's in charge of you.

"Now, that's some hair," Rose said with such a calm happy voice. "Reach down here and feel this hair."

I was hurting and at the same time I knew it was almost done and I reached down between my legs and felt the head of the stranger I loved and all of a sudden I pushed for joy and felt the shoulders then the whole body come out like if you're in a dream pushing hard against a door you've never seen before and can't help it and then it gives way and you fall into a new room.

Rose put her on my belly while she was still connected to me and then tied two shoe strings on the cord and cut between the two, and then it was done. She covered me and my wet baby and then sat waiting for my afterbirth to come out and while she waited I just looked at the person who'd been inside me all this time through all these things and my brain did not chatter a word.

"What you gonna call her?" Rose said while she did some things to finish up.

"Right now I'm not gonna call her anything. I'm just gonna look at her. Let her be. She's beautiful."

"Yes, Lord, yes, Yslea," Rose said. "That is one fine baby."

And while I lay there with no words and no thoughts I felt the memory of my own mama when she had me. I hoped she had a little joy.

The Blackness of Rose

I think delivering my baby girl took more out of Rose than it took out of me. She slept almost the whole next day, just waking to look at the girl and smile. She didn't eat or drink. I asked her if she wanted me to pull out her medicine bottles and she said, "No need for that."

So I knew she'd die soon, which was the only thing left to do. But it felt better now, like she had done this last piece of work bringing the girl into the world, and now the end could come.

I sat in Rose's old rocking chair with my baby. I still couldn't bring myself to name her. She didn't seem to need a name just yet. I couldn't see what she would do with it. I just looked at her and sometimes I seemed to catch her eye. She was really there. That was what I was doing when all of a sudden the room felt different and I knew Rose had died. For a time I didn't look away from my baby.

But then I looked at Rose. The shade of her skin was

almost the same as the shade of my girl's beautiful smooth black skin. I was afraid but not in a bad way. Say the skin is not named black or white. Say it is just looked at unnamed. Or say that Rose is not pronounced dead. No word spoken over her for just a minute. Just one quiet minute. Then what does it look like?

Black Rose dead, gone to heaven I think, and why not? I hope that much. But in the room just then, no words. But after a while you start to want to build a monument. To tell somebody who wasn't there what wonder is and why the room felt holy. So you have to start naming things. But not just then.

The blackness of Rose. Not some idea of Rose stuck in Memphis where black can mean all sorts of things that have nothing to do with you. But the blackness of Rose as she really was. The blackness that covers the shape of her faithful old body. Blackness like the blackness of my child with her perfect eyes, perfect nose, perfect mouth.

I love the tingling mystery of sneaking through a field on a black night. I love the clouds at night that hover over me like black angels with halos made of moonlight.

Everything except the surface of things is black. Black is the only color that is itself, with or without light. It is the color of the inside of things before they're torn open, when the mystery is still there.

The blackness of Rose's skin was heaped up in rich mounds where her wrinkles gathered around her eyes and on her neck. I thought to myself that so much beauty should not be missed by anyone.

If I think about the deep parts of the ocean I think in black. When I want to think of being alone for a time, as alone as I can be, I imagine being inside a closed silo in summer feeling cool stored grain like Joseph's grain beneath me, and every sound is an echo up the long cylinder above me, and I think it all in black.

But that's enough. I've had longer to think about the color black than any other color. I have felt the inside of it and I know it. I know its shades. I know its beauty and how it feels when people don't understand and use it to set others apart, to mark the ones who are set apart. I can be asked questions about the color black and I can answer them calmly and without getting upset, which is how I show that I really know a thing.

Baby. Child, I thought. As soon as I name you, you belong to the world. Other people can call you and when you know it's your name they're calling your eyes will turn away from me. You are the most beautiful thing I have ever seen, and the saddest.

I held her against my breast and looked at Rose. After feeling so full of this baby for so long I had wondered if I would feel empty. But I did not. I felt more full than ever, which was part of the silence so real and breathable.

I was almost ready to let words come back into the room like light beaming down the silo, fixing itself on everything, making everything show itself for what it is. I was almost ready to let words in but sat for a minute longer, waiting, feeling, happy. I did not hate anyone just then.

It was a great gift. To be in a place where so much comes together.

What It Was Like to Be Held

We all sat in three different worlds out on the porch. It's the way I think of it now and it makes me more ready to be kind to strangers. The baby I named Selah Rose for no reason other than that it is beautiful like she is, the only reason a name would fit her. Who knows what Selah Rose sees in the world or hears or smells that I don't? Thinking about what she feels that I don't feel made me stare at her with respect.

And Ambrosia. Mr. Piedmont knew a judge and the right thing happened. Lord have mercy. Sometimes since she doesn't hug or talk or look you in the eye I think her world is a small cold world like Pluto, an ice block too far from the sun to get any warmth. But then suddenly I just know that's not true. Her world may be small, as small as that book of colors but that also means there is nothing in her world except beautiful colors.

And they didn't know a thing about my world. They didn't know I hardly knew how to say thank you enough to Piedmont and Son for burying Layla and Rose. And they didn't know about worrying over money and the happiness at just having a little help. But then I went and did something crazy. But I feel good about it, almost like God is saying it's okay. I've always loved the astronomy magazine. I always seem to be the only person in the bookstore looking at it. But what I did is I took that five hundred dollars Jimmy left and I spent most of it on a telescope. Dimitri just sort of grunted when I handed him the money but I felt good walking out of there with the telescope.

Selah Rose and Ambrosia wouldn't have any idea what I'm doing staring into it. But in my mind it's like the silo I imagine when I want to be alone. In my mind it's the trip in the black treasure box, the storybook of everything.

I don't have as much chattering in my mind these days. I do a lot more watching and being quiet in my mind. But there is one thing that keeps coming back to my mind when I hold Selah Rose. And it's that at least for a while my own mama must have held me. She must have held me but of course I don't remember. Whoever I was then is as far away from me as who Selah Rose is. So in a way there are four of us.

I know enough about what it is to be scared. I look at my girl and wonder what it was like just to be held. Not to be afraid of men and women acting crazy on crack. Not to have to send my mind down past the grate into a fairy-tale world of dust and dropped things. Not to sit out back in the grass and look at the moon and wish to die, which no twelve-year-old should be made to wish.

Just to be held. Not even knowing how to think about trust. Having nothing to let go of. Just to be held.

I'd bet money my mama held me and wished all sorts of things over me and thought I was beautiful and also thought I was a sad thing because there was no way she could escape what she got into. I'd bet she said, "I'm sorry, baby girl. You're coming with me and I'm so sorry," even if she couldn't really think or say those words.

Me, who I used to be, Selah Rose, Ambrosia, Jesus. I think we'll be okay.

The World Bends When I Press My Eye

Selah Rose and Ambrosia are asleep. This is the time I give myself, when I sit in the bedroom listening to them breathe in their sleep and watch the way the light comes to me through Rose's stained-glass window, and I let my thoughts catch up with everything that isn't a thought.

Everything has changed. Jesus of course enjoys his morning nibbling grass and wandering around outside the window probably not too concerned with the way things have changed. Even though his name is Jesus he's still a donkey.

But when I think of going from asking for a glass of water to being the only grown-up left and with a new person around on top of it all, it's time to wonder at it all.

I look around at all sorts of things that will still be here when I'm gone. Things you can only see if you really look. Once you start thinking about it the world starts getting thicker. Everything has a story and every story if it's not told fast is just not gonna be told. But you can't tell every story about everybody and everything. And you can't tell every story fast. Some just have to be trusted to God's memory. You can't even tell every story about yourself to yourself. Some of it just has to be lived. But the memory of God, that's a comforting thought to me.

Men in rags, women trying to show what they've got and all they're really doing is showing what they used to have, men driving trains, rich men looking to the likes of Layla for something they think they can name but can't, Ambrosia's strange little world, Selah Rose's, mine.

The world gets so thick sometimes I can hardly breathe. Especially in all this heat. I notice a string of ants walking along the windowsill with their busy world bumping into each other, rubbing antennas, carrying crumbs, a piece of dirt, a dead ant. And I think of all the small worlds inside the large world inside the universe.

Even if you take all the magazines in all the racks and look inside for reports from different worlds, you've hardly started. Then add on everything that's ever been pulled in a train. Still barely started. Thick. Thick, thick, thick.

But then I press on my eye and the whole world bends. The ants blur. Jesus is crooked. The colored light blurs. I let go and everything straightens up. It's like everything I see could just drop away with the slightest push, a sheet blown off the clothesline in summertime.

I'm not sure if that means anything or not. But just as I start thinking about it there's knocking at the door and Selah Rose is crying. Ambrosia just sleeps through it but when that baby gets woken up and she's hungry, she'll let you know. She's not interested in how mysterious she is. She just wants something and she'll cry until she gets it, which makes me laugh.

I peek out to see who is at the door. It's Mr. Piedmont's son. His name is William. He has taken some interest in me, I'm not sure why. We're friends and he seems to enjoy it, even though I'm just me. I imagine he's seen just about everything with his job and there is never any telling what he'll say about the world, his thoughts are so solid and important. And that's why we can talk, sometimes for a long time if he has time and if I have time. But still he's so calm and strong in the knowledge of what he does. He's somebody I might ask about whether it means anything that the world bends when I press my eye. I expect he'll laugh. Even though he's a man who sees death every day he thinks it's funny that I want to think so much. He says he loves my thoughts and that makes me happy. He has a good sense of humor and he's very practical.

So when Selah Rose is crying and your friend William Piedmont is knocking on your door, it's time to put everything to the side and pick up the baby and answer the door. It's time to work in all sorts of ways. And it is enough.